A Touch of
CHRISTMAS

A Touch of
CHRISTMAS

TREASURED YULETIDE CLASSICS
FROM A MASTER STORYTELLER

GEORGE DURRANT

spring creek
BOOK COMPANY
Provo, Utah

© 2006 George D. Durrant
All Rights Reserved

ISBN 13: 978-1-932898-62-0
ISBN 10: 1-932898-62-X
e. 1

Published by:
Spring Creek Book Company
P.O. Box 50355
Provo, Utah 84605-0355

www.springcreekbooks.com

Cover design © Spring Creek Book Company

Printed in the United States of America
10 9 8 7 6 5 4 3 2
Printed on acid-free paper

Library of Congress Cataloging-in-Publication Data
    Durrant, George D.
     A touch of Christmas : treasured yuletide classics from a master storyteller / by
    George Durrant.
        p. cm.
     ISBN-13: 978-1-932898-62-0 (pbk. : acid-free paper)
     ISBN-10: 1-932898-62-X (pbk. : acid-free paper)
     1. Christmas stories. I. Title.

    PS3554.U694T68 2006
    813'.54--dc22
                            2006023582

Table of Contents

Publisher's Note

It is a pleasure to bring together in one volume these four Christmas stories written by George Durrant. For the past five decades, he has touched the lives of countless individuals through his numerous books, fireside speeches, religion classes, service as a mission president and in various LDS Church callings.

Through it all, George's love for the gospel has shined through, particularly in these Christmas stories. Three of these stories have been previously published, while *Christmas is for the Believers* is being published for the first time. We hope you enjoy them as much as we do.

Don't Forget the Star

A story of Christmas through the years
of childhood to parenthood

By George Durrant

Johnny wants a pair of skates; Susy wants a dolly;
Nellie wants a story book—She thinks dolls are folly.
As for me, my little brain isn't very bright; Choose for
me, Dear Santa Claus, What you think is right.

☆ Chapter 1 ☆

I Hope You Don't Get Everything You Want for Christmas

Without bragging too much, I'd say that I was better at making windmills out of Tinker Toys than any other kid in American Fork.

Of course, that might have been because I had so much practice. You see, nearly every Christmas from the time I can first remember such things I'd get a long, round box full of Tinker Toys. I recall one Christmas I wanted a scooter that had pretty good-sized wheels on both ends. You could hold on to a handle that came up on the front. Then you could put one foot on the scooter and put the other one on the ground and push off and away you would go. My friend had gotten one the year before and the two times he had let me ride it I had gone as fast as the wind. I couldn't wait to go lickety-split on that beauty out on the Alpine Road.

You can imagine my disappointment that particular Christmas morning when Santa Claus got confused and, instead of what I'd ordered, he left me another box of Tinker Toys. It was hard to

3

see how he could get scooters and Tinker Toys mixed up, but I guess he has a lot of orders and in those days there weren't any computers to keep things straight.

In an effort to make the best of things, I sat down and pulled the lid off the box and dumped those Tinker Toys out in front of me. In a few minutes I felt a whole lot better, because it's impossible to be unhappy when you are pushing a foot-long little wooden rod into a round hole in a little round wooden wheel. I must have made fifty different Tinker Toy contraptions before Mom told me that my oatmeal was ready. So, in spite of Santa's error, that still turned out to be a fine Christmas.

By the time December was about to roll around again, I'd lost interest in scooters. Remembering the mistake Santa had made the Christmas before, I didn't want to take any chances, so I ordered a little earlier. I did that by telling everybody, including my friends and my brothers and mainly my mom and dad, that I sure did want a Red Ryder BB gun. I mentioned it so often that my brother Kent said that he was sick of hearing about it and told me to shut up. My mother usually got after him for saying "shut up," but for some reason she didn't make a peep that time.

I still can't figure out what went wrong that Christmas. The only good thing was that the box of Tinker Toys was bigger that year and I could make a much fancier windmill out of those rods and little wheels. Besides that, this year those little flat pieces that you put on the ends to make the windmill blades were out of plastic instead of cardboard.

I had a lot of fun that Christmas day. Oh, sure, I'd be lying if I said I didn't feel bad. I still longed for the BB gun. Still, I had no resentment because it's hard to feel that kind of feeling toward somebody as good as Santa Claus. Besides, I knew that I'd get the BB gun the next Christmas.

Eleven months later, just two days before Thanksgiving, I was sitting in my classroom at the Harrington School, which was located just a block north of the downtown stores. We were drawing turkeys and pilgrims and Indians, but my mind was on the BB gun that I knew I'd soon be firing at just about everything in sight. With that thought filling up my mind from one side to the other, I was startled when I heard the 3:30 bell ring. Mom told me that I always had to be home by 4:00. But I couldn't wait to go down to Gamble's store and see if they had the Christmas stuff in yet. With that in mind, I headed south instead of north. About two minutes later I was walking along Main Street. I knew that if I walked faster than usual I could make up the lost time and still arrive home in time to meet Mom's deadline. Besides I wanted to be there in time to hear Terry and the Pirates and Jack Armstrong on the radio.

I hurried east along Main Street. Before I knew it, I was right in front of Gamble's store. I got so close to the window I touched it with my nose. As I was gazing in to try to see the BB gun, I saw something that made me decide I could live forever without Red Ryder's favorite firearm. There in Gamble's window was the fanciest bicycle I'd ever seen. I wish I could describe it. The word Hiawatha was printed in gold letters on that fat piece just in front of the seat. It was painted with a color somewhere between purple and red, with white on the tips of each fender. I had never seen anything so beautiful.

From the second I saw it, I started thinking about owning it. I doubt if anyone anytime anywhere ever wanted anything as much as I wanted that bike.

I stood there gazing in that window for a long time. Then I knew I had to head for home. I hardly knew where I was as I walked through the old mill lane. All I could think about was that Santa Claus had to be informed about my desires in such a way that he couldn't possibly get confused. We American Forkers didn't write any official letters to the North Pole, as far as I can recall. We just figured that if we talked about what we wanted to our friends and to our brothers and sisters and to our fathers and mothers that somehow Santa Claus would get the message.

It was hard to concentrate on Terry and the Pirates that night because I was thinking about that beautiful Hiawatha. It was two days to Thanksgiving. Then I'd have about thirty days to tell everybody I met that I was getting a Hiawatha for Christmas. If I talked about it like that for that many days I just knew that jolly old Saint Nicholas would surely get the word. To myself I said, "This year there'll be no mix-up." Then I added, "At least there'd better not be." Having said that, I hit my right fist down on the table to show that I wasn't just kidding around.

I never fell asleep for the next month without having that bike appear in the front part of my mind. I could see myself riding it up the Star Flour Mill hill without even having to get off and push. No kid in the history of American Fork had been able to pedal up that steep hill—I mean clear to the top. In my mind I could see Lelee and Dickie Hampton standing there watching me pedal by. They'd be as jealous of me as I'd been of them when they'd gotten to go to California the summer before. I could see myself riding up north to the canal and then coming back down so fast I'd be nothing more than a purple-red flash.

Finally the long waiting period was nearly over and it was Christmas Eve. It had always been hard for me to sleep on the night before Christmas, but that night falling asleep was as hard as trying to make a snowman in July. Somehow, after what seemed like a couple of hours, I drifted off into the Land of Nod.

It seemed like I'd only been asleep one or two seconds when I woke up. I could hear Dad taking the round metal lids off the stove so that he could put the newspaper and the kindling and the coal in. Hearing that, I knew it must be morning. I jumped out of bed and in the same sweeping motion I pulled on my overall trousers. As I hurried out of my room like a cowboy coming out of chute number one at the Lehi roundup rodeo, I could see the bike in my mind and I knew that Santa had come through. This time he'd kept the record straight. This time the bike would be mine. Without going to the bathroom or even hardly breathing, I hurried through the big kitchen that separated my back bedroom from our parlor.

I was so excited my heart was pounding faster than the motor of a Model A going up American Fork Canyon. I hurried past Dad, who had just struck a match to light the fire, and I entered the door to the room where I knew I'd see my bike near the Christmas tree.

In my haste to cross the room to find the bike, I nearly tripped over the biggest Tinker Toy windmill ever built. I looked straight ahead. There was no bike there. I turned and looked to the right, no bike; to the left, no bike; behind me, no bike.

I stood silently in the shock that comes when disappointed is just too weak a word. Then from behind me I heard the voice of my mother. "Look at this," she said excitedly. "Who could have built this?" I looked and she was pointing at the windmill.

My father, who had followed me into the room, spoke up and said, "I got up this morning and came in here and there was old Santa a-workin' on that. I talked to him and he said that he thought George was such a good boy that he wanted to not only give him a bigger-than-ever box of Tinker Toys, but also wanted to personally build him a windmill."

That was quite an honor, and a little bit of a desire to go on living came back into my heart. I walked over closer to the windmill. I'd had a few questions about Santa Claus lately because of what Bobby Jackson had said the week before during recess, but the windmill Santa had built proved that Bobby Jackson was wrong. I couldn't wait to tell the kids at school.

I'd be kidding you if I said I wasn't unhappy about not getting the bike. Yet at the same time I couldn't blame Santa. After all, he had built me a windmill. If he'd done that for every kid, he'd never have even made it out of Utah County that Christmas. I knew I must have been one of his favorites. I couldn't hold any ill will in my heart for him. Besides, I was already looking forward to the next Christmas.

I didn't want to take the windmill apart because of who had built it but I felt he'd be the first to understand if I did. There were a lot more pieces this year, and I built some amazing things.

Two days later I was sitting in my Sunday School class. The teacher was telling us about eternity being a really long time. I kept thinking, "Eternity might be a long time but it can't be as long as the time it takes to get from one Christmas to the next."

My New Year's resolution that year was to get the Hiawatha bike the next Christmas. When I went back to school after the time off for the holidays, Floyd Vest came riding to school on the Hiawatha bike. As I saw that, I started wondering a little about how fair old Santa really was. But then I remembered he'd built me a windmill. I talked to the other kids and he hadn't done that for any of them, so I felt sort of good, at least for a minute or two. But then I'd start thinking that I wished he'd built a windmill for Floyd Vest and then he could have been the lucky one who was Santa's favorite and I could have been riding the Hiawatha. Of course, it didn't matter much because I'd get the bike the next year. But I wondered if Santa knew how hard it was to wait from one Christmas to the next.

Winter was cold that year, spring came late, then the hot summer, finally fall, and then those wonderful days of waiting for Christmas. Slowly it was coming closer. Each day was filled with a little of the pain that always comes with waiting and a lot of the joy that comes from knowing that pretty soon something really good is going to happen.

Santa Claus—Loving, giving, disappearing. Here, there, where? He will be back someday. Santa Claus.

☆ Chapter 2 ☆

I Hope Losing Santa Made You as Sad as It Did Me

Finally it was just one week—seven days—until Christmas. The 3:30 bell rang and as usual I hurried out of the school and headed north on my journey home. Just before I got to the railroad tracks that ran along the north boundary of the school grounds, my older brother Kent called out from behind me, "Hey, George, hold up." I looked back and stopped and waited as he hurried toward me. Soon he was standing by my side.

We walked along together. For the next few minutes we didn't say a lot because we weren't friends—we were just brothers.

It had snowed a few days earlier, but it was a warm day for December and the sun had been out almost all day. The snow had melted off from the road and water was running along the sides. I liked to put my foot out to stop the little rivers of water and make ponds that would finally run over the tops of my shoes. I could tell I was getting the leather wet and I knew Mom didn't like me to do that, but it was fun and I couldn't help myself.

We'd walked about two blocks without saying anything. Then Kent, who was two years older than I was, spoke. "George," he said in a most serious tone, "look at all the houses on that side of this road." I did as he said and looked to the east side of the road where he was pointing.

He then continued, "That's a lot of houses, isn't it?"

I didn't reply, but I thought to myself, That is quite a few houses.

"Now," he said, "look at the houses that we are walking in front of."

I turned my head to the left and saw those houses. "There are a lot of houses along this street, aren't there, George?" he said.

"Yeah," I said, "I guess there are."

"And there are a lot more streets in this town and each one of them has a lot of houses on both sides."

I didn't answer because he hadn't really asked me anything. But I moved my head up and down in agreement because I knew he was right.

I was wondering why he was talking so much about houses but before I could figure it out he spoke again. "George, there are a lot of houses in this town and there are a lot of other towns in America and some of those towns are even bigger than American Fork."

I had almost always believed him because he was older than I was and he'd been to Colorado once. But I had a hard time believing there were towns bigger than American Fork. I'd been to Lehi and Pleasant Grove and both of them together could have fit in American Fork with enough room left over to build a baseball park.

While I was thinking about that, he added, "And besides America there are other countries like New York and Arizona and Europe."

I figured he was right in that because I'd studied geography in Miss Miller's class. I liked geography because I could spell it better than I could spell history or arithmetic. The reason for that was because Miss Miller had said, "Just take the first letters of these words and you can spell geography: George Edwards' old grandmother rode a pig home yesterday." I tried it and it worked. "G—E—O—G—R—A—P—H—Y." It was the biggest word I'd ever learned to spell. That's the reason why I'd pay extra attention when we studied all the places in the world.

Kent still hadn't made his point. "George," he said, "think of all the houses along this street."

I did that.

Then he said, "Now think of all the other streets in town." When he'd given me a little time to think about that he went on, "Now think of all the other towns in America and remember that some are bigger than our town. Now think of all the houses in other countries and add them to all the houses in America."

It was hard to walk along and at the same time think of so many houses. I was concentrating so hard I wasn't even having fun making dams for the water with my shoes.

Kent could see that my mind was chuck-full of houses. He stopped walking and I did too. He reached out and put his hand on my shoulder. Then he said, with the friendliest tone he'd ever used with me, "George, I have a question for you." He looked right at me and I'll never forget what he asked me because it changed my life.

"George, here is my question. How could one man, no matter who he is or how he can fly through the sky, or how many animals he's got pullin' him, in one night go down all the chimneys of all the houses on that side of the street?" He pointed to the east and then while he kept talking he turned and pointed west and said in a louder voice, "And all the chimneys of all the houses on this side of the street?" And then with arms outstretched he added, "And all the chimneys of all the other houses in this town?" He was speaking faster and faster as he said, "And all the chimneys of all the houses in America and all of the houses in all the world and do it all in one night?"

Suddenly and sadly I knew what he was saying. Bobby Jackson had tried to tell me but I wouldn't believe it. Maybe Santa hadn't really been the one who'd built the windmill. Kent smiled because he could tell I understood. I guess he figured he'd filled some kind of obligation. About that time he saw a friend up ahead and he shouted, "Hey, Lelee, hold on."

He ran off, leaving me all alone. I walked slowly and I kept looking down at the water on the sidewalk. I knew I'd just lost one of the best friends I'd ever had. I felt like crying. It was almost as if I could hear Santa Claus saying, "Goodbye, George. Thanks for believing in me and thanks for not ever getting mad at me even when you got Tinker Toys. And thanks for being happy even though you didn't get everything you wanted. And most of all thanks for being my friend for as long as you were."

Last of all, I thought I heard him say that he'd be back.

Teenage Christmas—Remembering, disbelieving,
longing. Empty, lonely, sad. Happiness of childhood is
behind and what is ahead? Teenage Christmas.

☆ Chapter 3 ☆

I Hope You Never Try to Cancel Christmas Because of Sadness

It didn't seem like it took as long for Christmas to come now that Santa Claus had gone away. For the first time in years I went right to sleep on Christmas Eve and I slept in until 5:00 in the morning instead of waking up early as I had always done before.

That year's Tinker Toys were in a bigger box than ever. Even so, the thrill was gone because I knew that not a single piece had ever even been in Idaho, let alone the North Pole. The windmill I made that year didn't seem to turn as easily as those of former years, and it didn't look as much like a real windmill.

The day after Christmas the north wind howled outside and the snow that had fallen a few days earlier was blowing into huge drifts. It was too cold to go outside to play. I stayed in the kitchen by the coal stove. It was the only place in the house where it was warm, except for when we'd build a fire in the parlor stove.

I had just built a drawbridge out of the Tinker Toys. I'd never been able to figure out how to do it before even though I'd tried every year. I was getting so I could figure things out better now

13

that I was older. I took the bridge apart and started to read a comic book. I had left the Tinker Toys on the floor. Mom was busy moving about preparing dinner. She stepped on a Tinker Toy rod and nearly fell. "George," she said, "pick those darned things up before I trip and fall."

When she said that, I silently agreed with her. They were "darned things." It was the first time I'd ever thought of Tinker Toys as being "darned things."

I knelt down on the linoleum floor and began scooping up the pieces. I had always liked the sound of Tinker Toys dropping into the box.

I soon had all the pieces in their round home. I walked to the side of the stove, reached up, and put the box on the shelf that was connected to the back of the stove up above where the coal was burning.

Mom was making potato soup, stirring it with a big spoon. She reached up for a salt shaker on the shelf where I'd put the Tinker Toys. As she did, she bumped the box and it tipped backward and then forward. Then it fell. As it did, the lid, which I hadn't put on very tight, came off. Nearly every Tinker Toy flew out and plopped into the soup.

Mom shouted excitedly, "George, get a newspaper!" I quickly went to the rack and pulled out last night's *Deseret News* and hurried to her side. As I held it with both hands she started fishing out Tinker Toys with her spoon. In about three minutes she got out what she thought was the last piece. It was then that she finally had time to be a little bit angry. If it had been one of the other kids who'd left those Tinker Toys up there, she would have really been upset. But I was her baby and it was hard for her to get very mad at me.

My dad was better at getting mad and he'd soon have a good reason to use this talent. A half-hour later we were all seated around our table having dinner. Dad was eating his potato soup when a shocked look came onto his face. We all sensed that he had encountered something unusual and we all stared at him. He lifted his finger and thumb to his mouth and pulled out one of the round Tinker Toy pieces that was about as big as one-eighth of a medium-sized potato. He slammed it down beside his plate and asked, "What in tarnation is this?"

Mother, who seemed as scared as a kid who'd broken a window playing ball, explained that a few of the Tinker Toys had accidentally fallen into the soup. Dad was only mad for a little while. Then I noticed he nearly smiled. "Please pass the Tinker Toy soup," he said. He usually wasn't one to compliment Mom on her cooking but he added, "That's just about the tastiest soup I've ever eaten."

That was my last year for Tinker Toys.

Because I was the last child in the family, I think Mom wanted to hold on to my childhood Christmases as much as I did. But that's like trying to reach out to hold on to the water of a river. The next year, a week before Christmas, she met me after school and we went to the back part of the J.C. Penney store to look at the toys. I tried to pretend that I didn't have much enthusiasm for being there. I was afraid my friends would see me there with my mom and ask me what Santa was going to bring me. That was one of the reasons that I quickly agreed with Mom that a magic set would be a good Christmas present for me. She bought it for me while I was standing right there with her. She said that she'd see that Santa would deliver it on Christmas morning. Hearing her say that right in front of the store clerk was as embarrassing as if she'd kissed me.

How can you look forward to Christmas when you know exactly what you are going to see under the tree when you get up on that cold December morning? At the same time, I'll have to admit I did like magicians and I'd always wanted to be one. I was eager to open that box and to start doing magic tricks.

* * *

I tried making the coin disappear but I couldn't do it quite right. Mom told me to read the directions again. I did, but I couldn't really understand what they were telling me to do. I hated to admit it, because I was a year older, but I missed my Tinker Toys. They worked just fine without any magic words.

There were a lot of feelings I had on that Christmas day that I didn't tell anyone about because I couldn't really explain them. Along about noon I thought to myself, "Christmas is a dumb day. It's nowhere near as good a day as Thanksgiving. At least you know that turkeys are real and you can count on them to never fly away on you." Besides, I liked the stuffing that Mom made out of bread crumbs. The yams were good, too. Even the cranberries were tolerable on Thanksgiving. But they'd make me queasy if I had to eat them on Christmas.

I started thinking that maybe even Halloween was better than Christmas. My friends and I would pull a lot of pranks on that night and nobody'd get mad at us because they wouldn't know who'd done it.

The Fourth of July was better than Christmas because of the parade, the ice-cold orange soda water, and the fireworks down at the ball park.

The only holiday that I could think of that didn't have Christmas beat was Labor Day. I remembered back to the last Labor Day. I was eating a delicious red watermelon slice with juice running down my chin. Dad said, "Be sure and spit those seeds all around so they'll grow and we'll have more melons next year." I laughed and was happy. It's hard to be sad when you are eating a watermelon. But then out of nowhere a terrible thought came into my mind. I remembered that the next day I had to go back to school. The rest of the day wasn't much fun at all.

As I thought about that, I decided it was all right to be sad on Labor Day because the next day school started, but to be sad on Christmas didn't make any sense. Thinking that made me all the sadder.

Dad was out feeding the chickens, Mom was in the kitchen cleaning eggs, and Kent had gone to play basketball with his friends. I was all alone, sitting in the parlor by the Christmas tree. Kent had given Dad a little silver metal toy gun for a present as a joke. It shot BBs, but wasn't any threat to the neighborhood birds because it had about as much power as a girl slugging you in the arm. And even with a dead aim you could barely hit the ground.

While I was sitting there feeling bad about feeling bad, I picked up Dad's gun and looked at it.

I shot it a couple of times at the cardboard lid of my magic set box, which was leaning against a chair. Then I looked over at the Christmas tree. I drew dead aim on a blue ornament hanging way out on the end of a branch about halfway up. Of course, I didn't shoot because nobody in all the history of mankind had ever shot a Christmas tree ornament. It just isn't right. It's almost worse than shooting a robin in the springtime.

I lowered the gun and was about to set it aside. The trouble was, I was so sad that I just felt like shooting at something. I raised the gun again, aimed right at the ornament, and slowly squeezed the trigger. It was almost impossible to even hit the tree with that gun, much less the blue ornament, but, incredibly, the ball exploded into hundreds of silver and blue fragments. I was shocked at what I'd done. Then, as luck would have it, Mom entered the room. I've never seen her look more startled. She turned from the mess on the floor and looked at me. I was still holding the gun. There was no use telling her I hadn't done it. Kent wasn't home, so I couldn't blame him.

She didn't get angry. She just looked at me for what seemed like a long time. I didn't want to look back but I knew that I had to. I could tell she couldn't believe that her son George could have done such a thing. I was wishing she'd get mad because I knew you couldn't be both disappointed and mad at the same time. The most painful thing that could ever happen to me was to have my mom disappointed.

I told her I'd pick up the pieces. She didn't say anything, just turned and walked out of the room, her eyes moist. In a few minutes I went in to where she was sitting in her rocking chair. I didn't say I was sorry again because she could always tell how I felt and she knew I was about as sorry as anybody had ever been. She reached out and held my hand. As I stood close to her, I felt that toys didn't matter much. The only thing that counted was not hurting people and doing good things instead of bad things.

Later that day I tried to pick up the pieces of the broken ornament and put them together with glue. I soon knew I couldn't do it, any more than I could put a broken egg back together. I finally gave up and just sat there. I hadn't cried in two years. And I didn't cry then. I wanted to, but I couldn't.

I decided then and there that that would be the last ornament I'd ever break. Just deciding that made me feel better.

I lay down on the floor on my back with my feet close to the base of the Christmas tree. I put my hands under my head for a pillow and looked at all the colorful decorations. I looked up at the star. It seemed more beautiful than it ever had before. As I was lying there, I wished I could go back to the way Christmas used to be. I felt that way because I remembered the happiness of the past, but at that time I didn't know anything about the joy of the future.

Gifts—Listing, shopping, buying. Make, bake,
wrap. The best of all are heart to heart. Gifts.

☆ Chapter 4 ☆

I Hope You Give Some
Unbuyable Gifts

The next few years my Christmases weren't anything to rave about. About all I can say for them is that they were better than not having a holiday at all.

Each year my friends and I would still go to the toy departments at Penney's and Chipman's and look at all the new toys. We'd act like we were making fun of the little-kid toys as we'd wind them up and scoot them along the floor. The clerk would say, "Don't play with the toys if you aren't going to buy them." We'd just smile and wait until he was gone. Of course, I knew I wouldn't get anything like that for Christmas because I was too old. Instead I'd just get a bunch of new clothes like socks and scarves and a coat and a toboggan hat and mittens. That excited me about as much as learning that the dessert at supper was going to be rice pudding with raisins.

The years went by slowly, but they still went by, and finally I was fifteen. That Christmas I told Mom what I wanted. I seemed to have more luck with her than I had had in the past with Santa. She followed my desires and I got a navy blue sweater that you'd pull over your head instead of buttoning. It was just like the one that Walter Bowen got from his uncle who went in the Navy. I also got a white sports coat. I put on that sweater and the white coat. There wasn't a speck of dirt on me and I looked pretty good. I couldn't wait for school to start so I could show up at the basketball game with Pleasant Grove in those clothes. If Louise saw me dressed like that, she'd really be impressed. Those clothes made that Christmas better than it had been since the end of the Tinker Toy days. It moved ahead of Halloween and the Fourth of July on my list of favorite holidays. But Thanksgiving was still number one with me.

When I was sixteen, Christmas made a bid to challenge Thanksgiving. That was the year Delmar Fraughton, my best friend, told me about mistletoe. But I must have stood under a sprig for two hours at the ward Christmas party, and all it did was keep the girls on the other side of the cultural hall. Thanksgiving stayed at the top of my list of favorite holidays.

Finally, I became a senior in high school. This was the year in which I was sure that all my dreams would come true. This was the year when I'd grow tall. This was the year when the girls would officially discover me. This was the year when I'd be student-body president. This was the year I'd be a bona fide basketball star for the American Fork High Cavemen.

But things were working out for me about like the presidential election worked out for Dewey. I didn't grow tall like I wanted. I still didn't dare put my arm around a girl and walk her down the hall. I wasn't a student-body officer. It was four days before Christmas and we'd already played six preseason basketball games—and I sure wasn't a star because it's hard to be a star if you're sitting on the bench. It seemed like none of my dreams was going to come true. I tried to be happy and I acted like I was happy and a lot of the time I was happy. But there was a deep corner of my heart that was hurting.

That night in practice I'd missed a couple of easy shots and the coach looked at me and shouted, "George, what's the matter with you?" When a coach asks that, it's almost as bad as having a girl laugh when you ask her to go to the junior prom. In the locker room after practice all the other guys were shouting. Delbert Hoaglund yelled, "We'll beat Lehi so far they'll all want to drown themselves in Utah Lake." But I wasn't saying anything because I knew that after what the coach had said I'd be watching the game from the bench.

Without even showering, I quickly dressed and headed out the side door of the gym into the cold December air. Over and over in my mind I could hear the words, "George, what's the matter with you?" I tried to answer that question to myself but I couldn't. It seemed like there was nothing really wrong except that everything was sort of wrong. It was dark already even though it was only 5:30. The snow was about six inches deep with a thick crust, and in most places I could walk on top of it without falling through.

I pulled my toboggan hat down over my ears and put my hands in the pockets of my plaid woolen coat. I walked as fast as I could. I crossed the snow-covered football field. I came to the edge of the school property. I walked up and down the old wooden stairs that the school had built to help us cross the wire fence.

As I headed down the steep hill just south of the Star Flour Mill, I had a fleeting thought that cheered my sad heart a little, and to myself I whispered, "I'll bet Mom will have a good dinner for me!" I don't know what I would have done in those days if it hadn't been for my mom.

Five minutes later with a near-frozen nose I was at the front door that opened right into our large kitchen. Mom was standing by the stove. Hearing the door open, she turned and greeted me with, "George, you must be half-frozen. Take your coat and hat off. We'll soon be ready to eat." She was standing at the stove, and I walked over to get a closer look at the pork chops, or the beefsteak, or the fried chicken. My heart sank as I got closer and discovered that she was cooking potato soup.

I usually tried to be nice to Mom because that's how she always was with me, but sometimes I was more ornery with her than I was with anyone else. I said in disgust, "Ma, why do you cook that stuff?"

"It's good," she replied.

"It's not good to me. You know that I like potatoes and gravy and meat. I practice basketball until I could drop and then I come home and all there is is a bunch of Tinker Toy soup."

"Well, your dad likes it."

"He might like it but I don't. Why don't we ever have what I like?"

"Oh, George, what's wrong with you? Lately it seems like nothing anybody does pleases you."

"Nothing's wrong with me."

Having said that I turned and went to the little washroom that was just through the door in the corner of the kitchen. There were some nails on the wall and I hung my coat and hat on the only two that were empty. I turned on the hot water to wash and warm my hands, and looked in the mirror above the wash basin. My hair had been pressed down by the toboggan hat. That plus my red nose and cheeks made me look discouragingly unhandsome. I pulled my comb out from my back pocket and tried to change things, but I knew it would take more than a comb. One of the things that was wrong with me was the way I looked. As I stood there, I shook my head from side to side with disgust. I don't recall any time when I felt more discouraged.

Mom came over near where I was standing and softly asked, "Guess what?" I didn't reply. She continued, "Your dad went downtown and got a Christmas tree today. He doesn't say much about it but I can tell he's as excited as a little kid. I asked him if he was going to decorate it or if he wanted you to."

Acting uninterested, I started out of the washroom. She stepped aside and I walked past her. I picked up the evening newspaper from off the top of the Singer sewing machine and sat in Dad's chair. I quickly turned to "Little Abner" to see if he'd been caught in the Sadie Hawkins Day race. The way I was feeling I thought Moonbeam McSwine had probably caught him.

Mom went back to stirring the soup. I was reading but I still heard her say, "Dad didn't say it, but I could tell that he wants you to decorate the tree."

"Why me?" I replied. "What's wrong with him? He's the one that bought the tree. I wouldn't care if we didn't even have a tree this year. He's never decorated a tree in his life. Let him do it."

"You know he won't. For years he's loved to watch you kids do it. Now everyone's gone except you. I know that he thinks you'll really want to do it. He even bought two new boxes of icicles and with your artistic talent you could make it very pretty."

"Artistic talent? I'm about as artistic as I am athletic."

"You can do it tonight, George."

"I'm not doin' it tonight."

"Why?"

"Because I'm going someplace."

"Oh, George, you don't need to go someplace every night. Why can't you stay home more?"

"Cause there's nothing to stay home for. It's Christmas time and I'm about as happy as the hunchback of Notre Dame. I want to go to the Owl Inn or somewhere and have some fun." Then I just had a feeling that I needed to blame someone other than me for my problems. So, as I often did, I blamed Mom. With a little bit of unkindness I said in a loud voice, "Besides, why did you ever name me George?"

"What do you mean by that? What's wrong with the name George?"

"George is a dumb name. Why didn't you call me Don like Afton and Marie wanted you to? If I was called Don, things would be different. Guys named Don get all the breaks. How are you supposed to amount to anything when you have a name like George?"

Mom seemed really shocked by what I was saying. Softly she replied, "George is a wonderful name."

"Not to me it isn't," I said, more determined than ever that my name was the basis for all that was wrong with me. To prove my point I continued, "You ought to hear the guys at school say, 'Hello, George.' The way they say it makes me feel about as bright as a burnt-out Christmas light."

"George, what's wrong with you? George is the best name in the world and it fits you perfectly."

"I know my name fits me perfectly and don't ask me what's wrong with me. I don't know what's wrong with me."

I wasn't reading any more. I was hurting inside and this was the first time I'd had a chance to tell anybody how I felt. I knew my name wasn't the real problem but that was something I could get at and Mom was someone I could say things to without worrying about it.

Dad was out putting the curtains down in the chicken coops. I knew we couldn't eat until he came in.

I started to read again because I had a feeling that all I was doing was upsetting Mom, and besides, what good would talking do?

Mom finished setting the plates on the table. Then she went back over to stir the soup. As she stood there, she looked at me and I looked at her. Oh, how I loved her and I wanted to go close to her and tell her I was sorry. But I didn't. She spoke softly, "George, don't you really like your name?"

I had had enough. I didn't want to say any more. "Yeah, yeah, I like it. Just forget it, will you?"

"Do you know why you're named George?" she asked.

I held up the newspaper and acted like I was reading. I didn't say anything to her, but whenever I was hurting inside I loved to hear her talk. It seemed as if her words weren't as important as the way she longed to make me happy.

She continued, "When I was a young girl, we lived out west of Alpine. There were no houses nearby and so I had no close friends and I was often lonely. My mother was sick and I used to care for her and my father and my little brother Steve. I didn't like living way out there away from everybody. I would go out to the stream to get buckets of water and I'd wish we had water piped into the house. Sometimes I would wish I wasn't so tall. Sometimes I was really unhappy.

"But through those lonely years I had an older brother who was the light of my life. He would often go away to the sheep herd. He'd be gone for weeks at a time. Then finally he would come home, and when he did, he'd always bring me a present. I'd look forward to his coming home more than I'd look forward to Christmas.

"One year, when I was about to graduate from the eighth grade, which was the last grade we had in Alpine, he made a special trip home so that he could be there with me.

"It was in the springtime and I knew the very day that he was coming. I watched for him, and the second I first saw him at the other end of the long road that led to our house, I ran to meet him. He got off his horse and gave me a hug and lifted me right off my feet.

"The first thing he said was, 'Marinda, I hear you're about to graduate. I'm proud of you. I was thinking you'd need a new dress to graduate in.' He then reached into his pocket and pulled out a gold piece. I'll always remember him handing it to me and smiling. It was one of the happiest moments of my life.

"Several years went by and I married your father. We had

eight children before you were born. Just two months before you were to come into the world my dear brother, still a young man, suddenly died. I was heartbroken and wondered if I could ever quit crying. In my prayers I told Heavenly Father that if you were a boy I'd name you after him."

Tears filled Mother's eyes. As I looked at her, she was hardly able to speak as she said, "His name was George." I'll never forget the way she said that name. I'd never heard it that way before. She wiped her eyes with her apron and her gray hair seemed to shine as she added, "That's why when you were born I named you George. To me the name George is the grandest name of all."

I don't know what it was about that story. Maybe it was just the way Mom told it. Maybe it was that I needed something special, or maybe it was just that it was so near Christmas. Whatever it was, I suddenly felt different inside. Mom wiped the tears from her eyes with her yellow apron and hurried to finish preparing dinner before Dad came in.

To myself I softly said, "George." Somehow it sounded different. I said it again, "George." I sort of smiled and thought, I like it. It sort of begins and ends the same way.

As we were waiting for Dad, I got to thinking about how glad I was that Mom's brother George had made her so happy. I got to wishing I could make someone happy. I thought, "The trouble with me is I don't have any gold pieces or any other kind of money."

About then Dad came in and we all sat down to the Tinker Toy soup. Dad didn't say much but I could tell he was pleased to have such a good meal. I took a big spoonful and as it hit my hungry taste buds I thought, "Mom makes the best Tinker Toy soup in American Fork. It must have extra ingredients." Oh, I'd still rather have had a pork chop and some fried spuds, but I had two bowls of soup anyway.

After dinner I looked in the mirror again and my hair had

straightened itself out a little. My cheeks and nose were the right color again. My eyes looked really brown and my nose even seemed shorter. As I combed my hair, I was thinking that, the way I looked, Louise might even accidentally on purpose try to arrive under the mistletoe at approximately the same time as I did.

Outside I could hear a car honk three times. I knew it was Lum Nelson in his dad's 1941 Chevrolet.

I opened the door and bounded down the three porch steps in a single leap. As I ran toward the front gate, I almost slipped on the ice-covered walk.

From behind me I heard Mom shout, "George, if you have to go, come back and get your coat."

A few seconds later I was back at the front door and then in the kitchen. Mom was doing the dishes. When I came in, she looked around and was startled to see me. "I thought you were going out for the night."

I smiled and replied, "I was but I changed my mind." Dad was sitting in his rocking chair reading the front page of the newspaper. I walked over and sat on the part of the stove called the reservoir, which is where the water used to be heated before we got the hot-water tank. It was warm there and it was a great place to sit on a cold night. Dad was not more than six feet away, so I could talk softly and he could still hear me. "Dad," I said, "I was thinking I'd like to decorate the tree you got. Mom said you even bought two new boxes of icicles. That ought to make our tree the best one in town."

Dad lowered the paper and looked at me. He didn't say anything but as he lifted the paper up again I thought I even saw him smile a little bit.

I jumped down from my warm seat and asked Mom if the decorations were in the box above the closet in the back bedroom. She said they were and in a minute I had them. Dad had already put a wooden stand on the tree and it was in the parlor just waiting to be decorated. I stood in the doorway that separated the kitchen from the parlor and before closing the door I said, "Don't you two come in here until she's all decorated."

I looked through our phonograph records until I found the one with "Silent Night" on one side and "O Little Town of Bethlehem" on the other. I found the crank and wound the Victrola up as tight as she'd go. I didn't want to have to wind her again until I'd finished my special mission.

Hanging two boxes of icicles on a tree takes a lot of time, especially if you are hanging each of them just right so that it dangles down straight for a foot or so. I wasn't in any hurry because I was about as happy as I'd been in years and I was singing, "Silent night, holy night." I sounded good enough to give Bing Crosby a scare. Every once in a while I'd softly say the name "George."

Finally the tree was nearly all decorated. I'd just moved a red ornament to where a blue one had been and the blue one to where the red one had been. I was standing back near the opposite wall so I could get a good look at the balance of my artistic labors. I was thinking so hard about what to do next that I was startled to hear my mom say, "George, your dad and I wondered why it's taking you so long." Then she saw the tree. "Oh, George, it's beautiful!" I was thrilled at how happy she looked. I loved it when I made her happy.

Excitedly I said, "I'll plug in the lights and she'll look even better." I crouched down and pushed the plug in. As I walked over to be near Mom and Dad, I could see the red and blue reflections in Dad's dark brown eyes. He didn't say anything but I could tell that he felt better than he would've if I'd just given him a gold piece. I'd never seen him look happier. I felt like a real George.

We all three stood there for a few seconds with the kind of feelings that you have when you are with your family and you're happy. Then Dad in his low and slow voice said something that I will never forget: "George, don't forget the star." I looked up at the top of the tree. Sure enough, I had forgotten it. I laughed and said, "How could I forget that?" I walked quickly to the bench, picked it up, stood on a wooden chair, and gently placed the star on top of the tree. Dad didn't speak but, as I looked over at him, he nodded his approval.

Usually one story from a mother to a troubled son doesn't change things as dramatically as I have portrayed. But many stories and words of love from a mother or a father to a child can over time bring about a miracle.

I don't remember what presents I bought for Mom and Dad that year. They couldn't have been much, for as I said I had little money. But I'll never forget that night when I stayed home and decorated the tree. I'll never forget that night when I made my mom and dad happy by giving them that unbuyable gift—the gift of myself.

I don't remember in much detail many of my teenage Christmases, but I remember that one because it was that Christmas that I began to dream not of what I could get but rather of what I could give.

Seldom is a war won in a single skirmish. Since that Christmas I have continually struggled against selfish desires. I continually try to answer in my own soul the questions of who I really am and what I can really give. But on that Christmas the seeds were planted that through the years would grow to the point where I could more fully give the gifts of my heart and in so doing follow Dad's words, "Don't forget the star."

*They looked up and saw a star, Shining in the East
beyond them far, And to the earth it gave great light,
And so it continued both day and night.*

☆ Chapter 5 ☆

I Hope Your Christmas Really Becomes Christmas

If on one particular day many years ago you had asked me, "George, what kind of Christmas are you going to have?" I don't think I could have answered without breaking into tears.

You see, that was the first time in my life that I had been away from home at Christmastime. And when you are your mother's baby like I was, being away from her and your family for the first time at Christmas is more than you or any person should ever have to endure.

In mid-November of that year, I had left the New York harbor aboard the great ship *Maritania*, bound for a two-year mission in the British Isles. After a seasick week I arrived in Southhampton, England. I spent a few busy and eventful days in London, and then received my specific assignment.

Now, as Christmas approached, I was in a city called Kingston Upon Hull. The excitement of travel had worn off and had gradually and completely been replaced by discouragement. I'd been in Hull, as it was called, just one month and I had been homesick since I'd arrived. As day by day and hour by hour

30

Christmas came closer, that most painful malady of the heart grew ever worse.

To add to my woes, the cold damp foggy air filled my lungs as, with my companion, I pedaled my bicycle for miles to call upon those who would listen to messages of the restored gospel. Under such conditions my nose began to run on December the twenty-second. I began to cough on the twenty-third, and on Christmas Eve I had an almost perfect cold.

As soon as I had arrived at my assigned area, I had written home:

Dear Mother,

My address is Elder George Durrant, 4 The Paddock, Anlaby Park, Hull, England. Please let all the family and all of my friends know that if they and you desire to send me Christmas cards and gifts they can send them to that address. Please call as many people and advise them of this as quickly as you can.

I hopefully supposed that this letter would get home in time for the returning mails to bring me some measure of Christmas joy.

Each day I'd wait almost breathlessly for the postman. He'd be laden with so many cards and gifts that instead of trying to slide them through the mail slot in our front door he would bang the brass door knocker. I'd throw the door wide and reach out and grab the entire pile. Surely at least one-half of these would be mine. With trembling hand I'd pull one from the pile and read. The first one was addressed, "Elder Tagg." The next one, "Elder Tagg." The third, "Elder Tagg." One after another the same name appeared. I was soon willing to settle for just one. But there wasn't one. In all, during the week before Christmas Elder Tagg received thirty cards and several gifts. As he'd open each card, I'd have to look away.

Finally, it was the last mail delivery day before Christmas. I had prayed fervently that I'd receive some Christmas greeting from home. The mailman came up the walk. The door knocker clanged. He reached out and so did I. To my joy there were seven cards and a small brown package. One by one I read the addresses and handed the first, the second, and finally all of the cards to Elder Tagg and then I tossed him the present. I could tell that he was deeply sorry and I knew that if he could have he would have given me any one or even all of the cards and the gift.

I turned away and ran up the stairs to our bedroom. I felt that I needed time to think. As I sat there on the side of my bed, I placed my coupled hands against my bowed head. I wanted desperately to somehow turn the clock and the calendar ahead and just skip Christmas. I knew I could make it through the other 729 days in England but I didn't feel that I had the power to weather this first Christmas.

As I sat in deep silence, the landlady, Nellie Deyes, and Elder Tagg came to the open door. She said, "Elder Durrant, I've come to say good-bye for a few days."

I looked up and she was looking away from me and I could sense that her heart was also heavy. "What do you mean, good-bye?" I asked in surprise.

Without answering she turned and was gone. Elder Tagg spoke softly, "They fear that she has cancer. She wanted to wait until after Christmas to go to the hospital but she just learned this afternoon that a bed has opened up at the hospital and so she must go now."

I was shocked. She reminded me so much of my mother and I'd grown to love her in the month we'd lived in her home.

I went downstairs to where she and her loving husband were just ready to leave for the hospital. I'll forever remember the look in her eyes as she said, "Elder Durrant, I love you. Now you be sure and have a good and happy Christmas." Then she asked if Elder Tagg and I would give her a blessing. Elder Tagg anointed her head with oil. As we both laid our hands upon her head, I poured my heart out to the Lord in prayer that she would soon be well. Later that night she went into surgery. Christmas Eve she died.

When I learned the news, I wanted to pray but I could not. I'd had so much love, so much hope, so much faith—and yet she had died. I wondered about many things that foggy Christmas Eve.

Sister Guest, the Relief Society president, had two weeks earlier invited all four of us who served as missionaries in Hull to come at noon on Christmas day for a goose dinner. On Christmas morning at about 11:00 the two other elders came from their home some four miles away to the place where my companion and I lived. The plan was that Elder Tagg and I would proceed on with them to the dinner. We were all greatly saddened by the passing of Sister Deyes but we knew that she would want us to go.

My cold had indeed worsened and the two elders who hadn't seen me for a few days commented on my apparent ill health. After discussing the matter with Elder Tagg we decided that I shouldn't go out into the damp air. Pop Deyes was at home and I said I'd stay with him. The others agreed and soon the three of them were gone.

Pop Deyes was in his quarters and wished to be allowed to remain in solitude, so I was left to myself in the front room. It was Christmas day and I was more alone than I'd ever been and more alone than I thought anyone else had ever been.

There were no gifts. There were no cards. There was no Christmas tree. There were no carols. There was nothing. The silence of the room was broken only by the mechanical working of the cuckoo clock. It was now just past eleven o'clock in the morning of the saddest day of my life and it was Christmas.

I moved closer to the fireplace, which was the only source of heat. The glowing embers seemed to be trying to act as my private

Christmas lights. Resenting their attempt to brighten my soul, I picked up the nearby metal poker and pushed at each one to crush out its glow.

I lowered my head and cradled it in my left hand. I sat that way until a "cuckoo" brought me back from where I had been. It was noon.

The room was growing colder now. I arose and poured some coal onto the few embers that remained. Now the fire didn't give off any heat because the new coals had covered the hot ones. I pulled my chair closer to the fireplace. Almost accidentally I looked on the mantel and there I saw my Bible. I stood and reached out and grasped it and sat back down. I really didn't want to read. I was far too sad to read. Yet at the same time, as a new missionary, I needed to know so much. The others knew so much and I seemed to know so little.

It wouldn't hurt to read a little—just a page or two. I opened the book beyond the middle and found my eyes focused on the words, "The gospel according to St. Matthew."

I didn't want to read. I wanted to be home. With clenched fist I hit the open book and then shook my head almost as if I could by saying "no" cancel every painful feeling that filled my sorrowed soul.

Because the pages were right in the line of my sight, I found myself staring at all the words at once. Without a conscious effort I focused on the first verse. I read, "The book of the generation of Jesus Christ, the son of David, the son of Abraham."

Like obedient servants, my eyes read the genealogy of Jesus, but my mind was not willing to let the words become thoughts. A few seconds later it was as if the words on the page forced my eyes to call my mind to attention. With full concentration I read, "Now the birth of Jesus Christ was on this wise: When as his mother Mary was espoused to Joseph, before they came together, she was found with child of the Holy Ghost."

Placing the fingers of my left hand at the bottom of this sacred verse I looked up at the mantel above the fireplace but I really wasn't looking at all. I wondered, "What does this mean? How did it say it?" I looked back at the page and read again, "She was found with child of the Holy Ghost."

I felt an incredible sense of wonder. Somehow, through a process beyond my intellect, I sensed that what I had just read was among the most important truths ever known. My eyes lifted slightly and I read the entire verse again, this time in an audible whisper, "Now the birth of Jesus Christ was on this wise: When as his mother Mary was espoused to Joseph ..." I paused and wondered, What does espoused mean? I read on, ". . . before they came together, she was found with child of the Holy Ghost."

Without looking at the verse I read again from the memory of my mind the words, ". . . of the Holy Ghost."

I knew I had heard all this before. But somehow I'd never really heard it with my heart.

To my mind my heart whispered, "So Mary is his mother, but Joseph isn't his father."

I noticed a small letter "i" near the words "of the Holy Ghost." I looked at the footnote and read "Luke 1:35." I rapidly turned the pages ahead and eagerly read, "And the angel answered and said unto her, The Holy Ghost shall come upon thee, and the power of the Highest shall overshadow thee: therefore also that holy thing which shall be born of thee shall be called the Son of God."

Letting the book rest in my lap, I touched my chin with my left hand and stared at the coals, which were just now beginning to turn from black to orange. Gently I whispered, "The Son of God." A surge of energy went up and down my spine as I felt my soul fill with light. In a louder voice and with pure knowledge I softly said, "Jesus Christ is the Son of God." That thought caused me to sit more erect.

With half a smile, I turned back the pages to Matthew.

I read on until I came to the words, ". . . the angel of the Lord appeared unto him in a dream." I wondered, "Are there really angels?" And within my soul I heard the glorious message, "Yes, there are angels."

A few seconds later I was in the midst of my own Christmas pageant. "Now when Jesus was born in Bethlehem of Judea in the days of Herod the king, behold, there came wise men from the east to Jerusalem,

"Saying, Where is he that is born King of the Jews? for we have seen his star in the east, and are come to worship him."

Again I let the book rest in my lap as my mind flooded with memories. I remembered when I had proudly taken the part of a wise man in the Christmas pageant. Because of that memory and the feelings of my heart, my face was now fully covered by a broad smile.

I read on, ". . . the star, which they saw in the east, went before them, till it came and stood over where the young child was.

"When they saw the star, they rejoiced with exceeding great joy."

As I pictured in my mind that holy star, I could see my mom and dad in the doorway looking in at the newly decorated tree. I could hear Dad's words, "George, don't forget the star." That thought caused me to sit and just stare at the glowing embers. Oh, how I loved my dad and mom—and for a few minutes I was at home with them.

I continued to read, "And when they were come into the house, they saw the young child with Mary his mother, and fell down, and worshipped him: and when they had opened their treasures, they presented unto him gifts; gold, and frankincense, and myrrh."

The fire was now giving off a great warmth but it seemed that the greater fire burned within me. For, in my soul I knew that Jesus

Christ was the Son of God, that he had been born in Bethlehem, that a star had shone over where he lay. As I continued to read, I knew that he was baptized in the waters of the Jordan, I knew that he was tempted of the devil but that he overcame all temptation. I knew that he was speaking and challenging me when he said, "Blessed are the pure in heart: for they shall see God." Oh, how I longed to be pure in heart! Of all the goals of life, I could think of none that would be so desirable as to be pure in heart.

As I read every page, paragraph, line, and word of the Book of Matthew, I could see and I could feel. As I read of his crucifixion, I remembered the words of the song, "Were you there when they crucified our Lord?" And I was, for as I read I was there and in my heart I trembled. As I read of his resurrection, I rejoiced. My soul was filled with hope as I finally read the last two verses of Matthew. I could almost hear his voice as he spoke directly to me:

"Go ye therefore, and teach all nations, baptizing them in the name of the Father, and of the Son, and of the Holy Ghost:

"Teaching them to observe all things whatsoever I have commanded you: and, lo, I am with you alway, even unto the end of the world. Amen."

Slowly I closed the book and with both hands I held it close to me. To myself I said, "Jesus Christ is the Son of God. There are angels. He did live and teach and love and perform miracles and was cruelly crucified and then he rose again. He is my Savior and this is his Church. I'm one of those he has sent forth. He is with me forever."

As I sat there holding my Bible, it was late on Christmas afternoon. Never had I been so happy in such an inward way. On that glorious day I had found the one who is the heart of Christmas.

I had found him when I felt forgotten by my family and friends. I had found him when I felt the pain of being away from home. I had found him when the death of someone I loved had torn at my heart. I had found him when I felt hopeless. I had found him because I'd followed the star. I had learned what so many have learned, that following the star, and never forgetting, is not always easy. Sometimes the nearer the star takes us to the stable and the garden and the cross, the more difficult the journey becomes.

That Christmas in England I learned that Christmas can be Christmas without a multitude of things. Mistletoe, colored lights, green-boughed trees, yule logs, greeting cards, and Santa Claus each have their own special way of gladdening our senses and delighting our hearts. But Christmas cannot be Christmas without Christ. On that holy day uncontrollable circumstances had pushed all else aside and left me free to follow the star. On that day I learned that Christ does not fit into Christmas. He is not part of Christmas. Jesus Christ is Christmas.

In the years since, I've learned that the pressures and selfish desires of life can push themselves between me and him. If I want to "not forget" the star, I must take the time to be alone with him. I must read of him, think of him, and pray to be near him. Then in the east I see the star. I follow it. I find him and when I do I feel free—free to let my soul soar into the realms of the sacred and indescribable joy that I found first in England many Christmases ago.

When the clock is striking twelve, When I'm fast asleep,
Down the chimney, broad and black, With your pack you'll
creep; All the stockings you will find Hanging in a row,
Mine will be the shortest one, You'll be sure to know.

☆ Chapter 6 ☆

I Hope Santa Comes Back to You, Because He's Not Just for Kids

After returning from England I hoped that I would never again forget the star. Yet I still longed for the good old days when Santa Claus was at the center of the fun side of Christmas.

Jolly old Saint Nicholas had been missing from my life for over fifteen years.

He'd been gone so long that I really didn't know where to even begin to try to find him. I considered contacting Mr. Keen, the tracer of lost persons. When as a young boy I had listened to him on the radio, I had thought he could find anyone. Perhaps he could help me locate my former friend. But I didn't even know how to locate Mr. Keen. Anyway, I sensed that was not really necessary. I knew that if I was willing I wouldn't really have to find Santa Claus. I knew that if my heart was right, he'd find me.

I realized that to prepare myself for such a happy reunion there were certain requirements that I had to meet, centering around the exciting adventure of having a family of my own.

As I had grown up, I had wanted to be a basketball star, then a great missionary, but never before had I wanted to be anything so intensely as I then desired to be a husband and a father. Having long had such a goal, and with my mission to England now behind me, I was more than willing to enter such a venture. As a matter of fact, I was not only willing, I longed for and dreamed of a little home, a wife, and wall-to-wall children.

I had met Marilyn while she and I served our missions at the same time in England. We had kept all of the mission rules. However, I did have an electrifying handshake. Marilyn had returned home in September and I had arrived back in mid-December. We had seen each other often since my return.

The day before Christmas I borrowed my dad's truck and drove to downtown American Fork. I parked and walked toward Garth Reed's jewelry store. I pulled my wallet from my pocket, opened it, and looked at the small number of green bills that were inside. To myself I whispered, "Oh, Santa Claus, how I could use you now! Between the two of us perhaps we can get the size of ring that Marilyn really deserves."

I guess he was busy packing his sleigh, because he was about as much help to me on that occasion as a skeptical banker. Anyway, a few minutes later I walked out of the store with the finest Christmas present I'd ever purchased. As I pulled the truck door shut and pushed on the starter, I said to myself, "If Marilyn accepts this, I'll know that giving is indeed far better than receiving."

That night, Christmas Eve, I borrowed my brother John's car and headed up around the Point of the Mountain and on into Salt Lake City. I went straight to Marilyn's house. I was so excited I could hardly speak and that was all right with her dad because he was watching TV.

We went out to dinner and I was so beside myself that I could hardly taste the meat in my Dee's hamburger. After eating our final french fry we drove up State Street. I stopped the car near the State Capitol Building. As we looked out at the lights of the city, we talked for a few minutes. I couldn't concentrate on anything but the ring. Being with Marilyn was like having a lot of my dreams coming true and a lot more being ready to come true. I was absolutely certain that she deserved the very best and the time seemed right, so I pulled the small box from my pocket and placed it gently into her hand. With observable excitement she opened it and pulled the ring out from the satin slot in which it rested. Then she looked up and over at me. I could tell she was pleased and that the answer was going to be yes.

After a few seconds of silence, while we both looked down at the ring, we lifted our heads and looked deep into each other's eyes. I could see a reflection there. I could see the reflection of the stars of the northern sky. Then suddenly I saw something that I could scarcely believe. There in that amazing reflection I saw, crossing between the stars, some strange sort of vehicle. It was being pulled by several small animals, each of which seemed to have some sort of horns. There in the airborne apparatus was riding someone dressed in red. As far as I could tell, he had a white beard. He was waving right at me and even though he was about two and one-half miles away I could somehow read his lips as he shouted, "George, George, I'm back."

Desiring to see this wondrous sight more directly, I turned quickly, opened the car door, and jumped out. But I was too late. By now whatever it was that I had seen had passed behind a mountain peak and appeared to be headed toward Park City.

Marilyn was surprised at my strange behavior. A minute or two later when I got back in the car, she asked, "What did you see?"

Not wishing to appear irrational, I replied, "Oh it was . . . just a flying saucer." I didn't say anything more to her at the time. I was fearful that if I told her the truth she might think it so strange that she would change her mind about accepting the great gift that by now she had placed snugly on her finger.

Even though I said nothing more at the time, I knew that through Marilyn and the children that I prayed would come, Santa Claus had returned to my life. This time he was bigger and better than he had been before. This time he wouldn't be someone to get things from but instead he would be someone to give things through.

As we drove home that night, I became very silent. Marilyn touched my arm and asked, "What are you thinking about?"

I replied, "I was thinking about all the houses in American Fork and all the houses in Asia and Europe."

She looked at me as if she feared I was not of sound mind. But before she could speak I continued, "Maybe there is a way that he could do it. If he had help, I'll bet he could do it all in one night." Then, after pausing to consider the probabilities, I spoke again, "I know he could, if every father and mother gave him a hand. I'm willing. How about you?"

"Sure," she replied. "Sure." After a few quiet moments she added, "Speaking of houses, I guess you know you passed mine three blocks ago!"

"Of course I know. Santa and I, we know where every house is."

As I made a U-turn, I said, "You know, Marilyn, my brother Kent was wrong. His logic was right about the difficulty of the task but he failed to consider one vital factor." Before I could say more, we were at her house and the time for philosophical discussion was over.

I realize that you may be a bit skeptical about what I really saw in the sky above the State Capitol Building on that Christmas Eve many years ago. I'm sure you would say, "Now, George, we realize that you were too much in love to have really known what you did or didn't see." Then you might continue by saying, "We don't doubt that you saw a reflection, but a reflection isn't reality."

Well, you can believe what you want. But I've got more

evidence than one brief sighting to prove my point. I've got twenty-five years of very strong circumstantial evidence. Let's just take one of those years and look at it carefully. You'll have to give up your own Christmas Eve plans and come back in time with me to a December the twenty-fourth when my children were clustered around their early years. Come into my home and just stand back and watch. I guarantee that you'll see things that will remove all your agnostic thoughts about Santa.

You'll see me come home from work and come into the house. The children will come running to greet me because I'm very popular at home. You'll hear Matt shout, "It's Christmas Eve. Santa Claus is coming tonight."

Kathryn will gleefully add, "Yeah, and he is bringing me a Betsy Wetsy doll."

I'll hold Devin on my lap and ask, "What's Santa going to bring you?"

"A garbage truck," Devin will answer with joy.

"We'd better hang up our stockings," Marinda will say.

"You're right," I'll answer. "Santa has a lot of good stuff for us. So let's hang up big ones."

Dwight will pull at my hand and say, "Dad, tell Santa to put my stuff all on this chair."

"Okay, and where should he put your things, Warren?"

"Over in this corner," Warren will answer.

"When will Santa get here?" brown-eyed Sarah will ask anxiously.

"Not until we are all in bed asleep," I'll reply.

By now you'll see that I'm so excited I can hardly control myself. Little Mark will say, "I've been a real good boy so I'll get lots of stuff from Santa Claus, won't I, Daddy?"

"You sure will, Markie. You sure will."

Marilyn will say, "It's time for our Christmas pageant. Santa is important, but who is much more important?"

"Jesus," Matt will reply.

"Yeah, Baby Jesus," Kath will add.

Then you'll see a pageant at our house that you'll have to admit is the best you've ever seen.

"Now it's time to go to bed," Marilyn will say with obvious delight.

Soon you'll see the children all dressed in their pajamas. We'll ask you to kneel in prayer with us. We will feel a real closeness as we pause to give our thanks to him who makes family happiness the best happiness of all.

Then you'll watch as the kids head for their rooms.

You can come with me as I go to the bedrooms. "He'll be here soon, Matt, so try to go to sleep," I'll say.

"You didn't give me my kiss," Marinda will call out.

"Mom and I sure do love all of you. We are so glad that Santa is coming. I can't wait until morning. How about you?"

A few hours later the real evidence will be there for you to see. But you'll have to get up early to see it. Don't worry about waking up. I'll wake you because I'll be awake long before daylight.

When morning comes, I'll show you a place to stand near the bottom of the stairs. From there you'll be able to see perfectly.

A few minutes later you'll see the children come down the stairs or the hall. Be sure to look at their eyes. That is where the real evidence is.

Then watch as they move toward the place where the toys are. You'll see Santa as you've never seen him before. But you'll do more than see him in their eyes. You'll feel him in your heart.

The last evidence of all will be to look at me. You'll see a surprise in my expression that will be the conclusive evidence. You'll ask, "George, you seem amazed at what has gone on in this room since we all went to bed last night."

I'll reply, "Of course I'm amazed. Aren't you?"

Then you'll just have to admit, "I sure am, I sure am." And you'll know that there is only one conclusion. Somehow, some way, Santa has been there.

The evidence will be overwhelming. You'll know that what I saw up by the Capitol was real. There really is a Santa Claus. A Santa who knows that one of the happiest things we can do at Christmastime is to give something to someone without telling him who gave it. A Santa who long ago volunteered to be the one to take the blame for seven million and sixty-three Christmas mysteries each year. A Santa who agreed that on Christmas morning when parents say, "We didn't give it to you, Santa Claus did," he'll just wink and smile and won't say a thing. A Santa who enjoys getting the blame for things that make Christmas a time for little ones to have a full measure of Christmas joy.

Christmastime—Partying, shopping, wrapping,
Scurry, hurry, worry. Stop! Let meaning settle in
your heart. Enjoy some Christmas time.

☆ Chapter 7 ☆

I Hope You Have Some Real Christmas Time This Christmastime

Each chapter of life is better than the last one. And the heart of each year's experience is Christmas. It comes a lot more quickly now than it used to. It's no longer an eternity between one Christmas and the next. It seems that nowadays time has been speeded up. Christmases are like airplanes at a busy airport—they are all lined up just waiting to land.

The trouble is that they come so fast and there is so much to do that often at Christmas we are so busy that we don't take the time to have some real Christmas time.

As I think back and try to analyze things, the best part of my Christmases has been those times when I've slowed down and taken time to just sort of think about things. That kind of thinking and feeling time is best described as true Christmas time.

In England on that Christmas Day many years ago, I had more than a half-day of pure Christmas time—time to read, to think, to pray, to feel a closeness to him who was born on that first Christmas.

I had some Christmas time this past Christmas, too.

It was two Saturdays before Christmas. Thanksgiving—my second favorite holiday—was over and there was a lot of Christmas in the air.

It was time for the annual Christmas tree purchase. Marilyn and I don't go together to buy the Christmas tree anymore. I always want to buy the first tree I see and she can't bear to buy one until she sees the very last one. Things just didn't work out and so now she bakes cookies while I go for the tree.

This year I took my young son Mark. As we prepared to leave the house, Marilyn's last words were, "Don't buy the first tree you see." That would have been good advice for a less inspired man than me.

I just felt impressed to go to a certain Christmas tree sales lot. Once in the lot, I saw thousands and thousands of trees. I stood silently for a few seconds and then I was impressed to walk forward, turn right, then left, then back right, then ten paces ahead, and there it was—the perfect tree. (I wish I could do as well on used cars.) It seemed to cry out, "I'm the one."

"That's it, Mark," I said.

"It's a good one," he agreed. "But," he added, "Mom said to look around before we chose one."

"I know she said that but how was she to know we'd find the perfect one right off?"

By now I was walking to the front of the lot to pay the young man. "Mighty pretty tree," he said as he nailed it on a wooden stand.

I thought, "Of course it's pretty. I'm inspired in these matters."

As we drove home, I sang a few words of "O Christmas Tree," but Mark turned on the radio like the kids always do when I sing. I quit singing, turned down the radio and said, "Mark, about this tree."

He looked over at me as I continued in a most serious tone, "When your mother asks how we picked it out, why don't you say, 'We went to 47 different tree lots. We looked at 4,752 trees and finally after comparing each of those we chose this perfect tree.'"

His reply was, "That's not true." When I heard him say that, I found myself almost wishing that he'd not paid so much attention to all the Sunday School and Primary and home evening lessons on honesty.

We got the tree home and Marilyn was pleased. She didn't ask if I'd looked around before buying it. She knows enough about me that she doesn't ask many questions anymore.

She didn't even seem to pay any attention to Mark's indicting statement, "Dad bought the first one he saw." I felt like not getting him his electronic game for Christmas. But that would have deprived me of a lot of fun, so I quickly forgave him.

Marilyn asked, "How much did the tree cost?"

I replied, "I got this wooden stand for nothing. The young man even nailed it on for no charge." I then picked up the tree by its stand, told Mark to grab the pointed end, and we marched triumphantly into the front room.

I turned on some Christmas music, backed off, turned around, crossed the room, and sat down in a soft rocking chair.

My task was over. Now it was time for Marilyn and the four children who were at home to go to work.

The box that contained the ornaments, electric Christmas lights, silver rope, and some used icicles was opened. While I watched from my most relaxed position, the decorating began. I heard words like, "A little higher, a little lower, good, just right." I watched admiringly.

As they worked, I listened to everything from "Rudolph" to "Silent Night." I felt feelings of looking forward, of looking back, of love, and of pride. Laughter and love filled the air. It's hard for me to imagine a room ever being more jam-packed with Christmas.

Finally the last tinseled icicle was hung. Without leaving my chair, I shouted, "Pull the drapes so it will be darker in here. Then plug in those lights and let's have a look."

A few seconds later the only word I could utter was the best adjective of all, "Ahhhhh!" There is something so special about the first look at the year's freshly decorated tree.

A few minutes later we were gathered at our round table for lunch. As I sat there with my family, I wondered if there ever had been a richer man than I. I looked at the food before me on the table. I supposed to myself that only in rich families like ours would each family member have a different-colored drinking glass. Only rich families like ours would have hamburger all mixed in with macaroni.

As we were eating, I asked Marilyn to please pass me the margarine. She replied, "Call it butter."

"I'm too honest," I responded.

Sitting there with my family it was almost as if I could hear a pounding on our window. I knew that if I opened it, I might be knocked off my chair by a current of Christmas blessings coming from God and pouring into my home and into my heart.

About that time my little black dog, whose official name is "Little Dog," seemed to sense my happiness. In his own way he begged me to take him for a walk down the lane that leads along the foot of the mountain.

I was glad to grant Little Dog's wish because that path along the mountain is among my favorite places. It's one of the places where I like to go when I want to be near the source of all joy.

That December day was briskly chilly, but with my coat buttoned tight and my earmuffs in place, I was comfortable. As we walked along, Little Dog would leave my side and dash into the oak brush and around each sage bush. Then he would come back to the path to thank me for bringing him to such a dog paradise.

When I walk, my mind often fills with wonderful thoughts. And this time of year I couldn't seem to think fast enough to include all that clamored to enter my mind.

Soon I was passing in front of the old machinery that had once been used to pull gravel from the mountain.

In about twenty more yards I came to my favorite praying and thinking spot. I stopped and stood very still. Little Dog looked up at me and then darted off to search for grey birds. I turned and faced the steep slope of the rugged Mount Olympus. Starting at the lower ridges, I slowly lifted my eyes to the top. I love the mountains, for they cause me to look up. Somehow they give a feeling of strength and hope to my life.

Little Dog seemed to understand my need to be alone and he romped higher and higher up the slope.

I turned back and gazed at the great valley. I began to pray. I can't describe all that I said—some with words and some with silent thoughts. I didn't really ask for anything. My main desire was just to thank Him who made Christmas.

I recall that as I looked down at all the houses I remembered my brother Kent's words, "How could one man in one night ..." I smiled and chuckled to myself. Life had been good to me. I was so glad my mom had been my mom and my dad my dad. I was so glad I had grown up when and where I did. I said softly, "I wouldn't trade places with anyone in all the world." I looked up into the clear blue sky and thanked Him for it all.

I remembered the toy gun and the broken ornament. I had promised I would never break another one and I hadn't. There is so little bitterness about past follies when we know we have changed our ways.

In my mind I remembered all the things that can be built with Tinker Toys. I wondered why the directions that showed how to make a thousand things never once mentioned how to make Tinker Toy soup!

I remembered the feelings I'd had in England when all of what I had thought Christmas was had been taken away, and how that had freed me to find out what Christmas really was. I realized again that following the star was not something to be done only once, but that the journey must be taken over and over again.

There on the base of the mountain I felt I was finding Him again.

I remembered again the night I decorated the tree for my dad. I could see how he and Mom looked when they saw the tree. I could hear Dad's voice saying, "George, don't forget the star."

Through the years I've heard much of the spirit of Christmas. There on the mountain I felt every degree of that spirit and my soul vibrated with joy.

Suddenly I felt an urge to hurry home. I wanted to be with my family. It's good to be on the mountain but it's even better to be home.

As we walked along, my neighbor shouted out from his porch, "Merry Christmas."

"Oh, yes," I replied.

I was so glad for Santa Claus and Christmas trees and shopping, baking, and sending cards. All were part of the season. But most of all I was grateful for the sacred time—the Christmas time.

A few minutes later Little Dog and I were home. The tree was up. The star was on top. The gifts were made, the cookies baked. I was ready for Christmas and I was happy.

Christmas is for the Believers

By George Durrant

♣ Chapter 1 ♣

The Babe

S yd Bush was the biggest Yankee fan in the Midwest town of Rooster Creek and maybe in the whole world. Babe Ruth, "the Bambino," was almost a God to this man who lived for October and the World Series. His joy rose to its highest heights in 1927 when "The Babe" hit a record sixty home runs during the regular season and then led the Yankees to a four-game sweep of the World Series.

A week later Syd's wife, Marie, gave birth to an eleven-pound fourteen-ounce baby boy. Syd was nearly as happy over his newborn son as he had been with the World Series. For nearly two weeks Marie fought to overcome Syd's insistence that the child be named "Babe." She prevailed with the argument that the name Boyd was similar to the name Babe. Finally Syd agreed but he never called his son any name other than "Babe."

The Depression of the 1930s was a time of few jobs and little hope, softened for many only by focusing on the never-ending excitement offered by sports. Although few dreams seemed realistic during those discouraging years, Syd had a dream he knew would come true. In his mind he had a firmly fixed vision that his son would be the best player that baseball had ever known.

The boy was called "Babe" not only by his father but by all the sports-loving men of Rooster Creek, and by the time he reached his early teen years it was clear that he was indeed a natural ballplayer. Young Boyd Bush spent many hours with his dad catching, pitching, and hitting, in addition to watching the Rooster Creek team beat Provo, Magna-Garfield, and the other Industrial League teams of the 1930s and 1940s. Every conversation between father and son centered on what young Boyd could do to get ready for the major leagues.

There was no question that Boyd loved baseball. Nevertheless, he always listened, enthralled, whenever his mother played the violin. Marie even confided that she had once longed to play in Carnegie Hall. She would let Boyd hold the old instrument and show him how to draw the bow across the strings. But that came to a sudden halt one day when Syd came home from his job at the sawmill and saw thirteen-year-old Boyd with the violin in his hand.

"I never want to see that kid with that thing again!" Syd shouted at his wife. "He has more important things to do."

Even World War II did not dampen Syd's dream of his son being a major leaguer. Syd himself could not serve in the military due to the injury he suffered during a game that ended his own dream of being a big-time player. So during those years, he and Boyd spent every spare minute down at the ballpark practicing.

Seeing that Boyd's school work was entirely secondary to him, Marie, a well-educated and refined woman, tried to encourage her strapping son to study more. But Syd felt his son's ticket to the future was on the playing field, not in the classroom, and did not encourage Boyd to work harder in school.

As a teenager, Boyd was taller and had broader shoulders than the other boys his age. His strong chin, blond curly hair, and blue eyes drew attention from all the girls at school. Year after year, Boyd's size and his skill increased. His home run record in high school made him a legend in all of Utah County. The local citizens claimed that their "Babe" hit line drive homers that kept the cottonwood trees beyond the fence in right field trimmed of leaves and branches.

On Sundays, Boyd always accompanied his mother to Sunday Services. Although Syd claimed not to be a religious man, nothing could keep Marie from church on the Sabbath. Boyd liked church, and his favorite church stories were those of the miracles that could happen through prayer. He loved the stories of David slaying Goliath, and Moses parting the Red Sea.

Although Marie couldn't get her husband to church, she insisted that the family say grace at each meal and that they all kneel in prayer as a family before going to bed. Syd didn't seem to mind this practice and even told his son that when he went up to bat, he ought to say a silent prayer that he would hit a home run. Boyd hit enough home runs that he came to have an almost superstitious belief that prayer was as necessary to his powerful hitting as knocking the mud out of his cleats and taking his hat off and running his hand over his hair to smooth it down.

World War II ended just before Boyd's senior year. The happiness everyone felt at the war's end manifested itself in even greater enthusiasm for sports. That year the Rooster Creek Cavemen went undefeated in regular season play, and Boyd "The Babe" Bush was the town hero. After the game Boyd was often interviewed, and the local and state reporters always asked the same question: "What's the secret of your amazing success?" Each time Boyd's answer was the same: "Before I take the field and each time I go up to bat, I ask God to help me. He has never let me down yet."

Boyd became known as "God's power hitter."

All the young boys in town wanted to be like Boyd and began praying just like he did. Even the bishop gave a talk in church commending "The Babe" for his faith in prayer. Marie, hearing her boy called "The Babe," glared at the bishop who blushed then continued, "Uh... I mean, Boyd." But Boyd didn't mind. He loved to hear these things almost more than reading about his home runs in the sports pages of the *Deseret News*.

In post-season play Boyd's team easily defeated the Delta High Rabbits in the quarterfinals and the Murray Smelterites in the semis; Boyd hit two homers in each of these games. Now Boyd and his Rooster Creek teammates were to face the dreaded and hated Grantsville Cowboys. The year before, Grantsville had defeated the Rooster Creekers on a series of at least ten bad calls by the umpire, who later admitted that his nephew played with the Grantsville nine. Even worse, Boyd had the flu so he hadn't played his best.

This year the team and the town were determined to have their revenge. The game would be held at Rooster Creek, and the umpire, who wanted to be a county commissioner, knew he'd need Rooster Creek's votes to get elected. Never had there been such excitement in Rooster Creek. Syd even told his friends at the pool hall that he was more excited about this game than the upcoming World Series.

On the day before the championship game, a rumor spread through town that a scout from the New York Yankees had checked into the Green Row Motel and was there to see "God's power hitter" knock a few out of the park.

That night, when Syd stopped to fill his car with gas at Kelly's Service Station, Leonard Kelly told him that the scout had been in the station and filled his car with gas not more than fifteen minutes earlier. Syd could scarcely stay within the speed limit as he drove home to report that the Yankee scout was sure enough in town. When Boyd heard this he asked his mother and father to add their prayers to his. He wanted—more than anything he had ever wanted—to someday play for the Yankees. He assured his parents that he would be praying as never before that he would live up to his reputation as God's power hitter.

Finally it was game time. After warm-ups Boyd hurried to the outhouse where he could be alone. There he prayed, "Please, God, this is the time more than any other that I need your help. Please, help me to play better today than ever before." Then, filled with confidence, he took his place in center field.

In the first inning, the other team went three up and three down. Boyd's team went to the dugout, and the first hitter went up to bat. He struck out. So did the second hitter. Boyd began to study the pitcher more closely. He had heard that this southpaw pitcher named Snaker had moved to Grantsville from California at mid-season and that he had a mean curve ball. It was obvious that this guy was pretty good. Nevertheless, Boyd felt certain that this newcomer would be no match for him. He was ready to face the pitcher.

The next batter was hit by the pitch and limped painfully to first base. At last it was Boyd's turn at bat. He took a deep breath and shook out his muscles to relax. From behind him he heard the catcher shout to the pitcher, "Easy out! Easy out!" The pitcher chuckled and then his eyes narrowed as he glared at Boyd.

The crowed sensing the drama shouted, "Kill the Snake! Knock it out of the park!" Boyd forced a smile to his face to unnerve the big lefty. The pitcher hesitated too long before going into his windup, and Boyd called time and stepped out of the box.

Boyd then knocked the dirt from his shoes, and took his red cap off to push his hair back with his hand. Putting his cap back on, he headed to the batter's box. The crowed cheered with joy as their hero stood close to the plate. Boyd uttered a swift, silent prayer as he watched the lefthander wind up. The ball seemed to bend as it sailed in. Boyd stood motionless as the ball thumped into the catcher's mitt.

"Ball one!" shouted the umpire. Boyd stepped back from the plate and took a deep breath before moving in for the next pitch. The next few minutes were the worst of Boyd's life as he heard the umpire shout "Strike!" not just once but three times as Boyd's bat missed the ball each time.

In disgust but not discouragement, Boyd threw his bat over

to the dugout and ran toward center field. "It's all right," he told himself firmly. "Next time it will be different."

But it wasn't different. Again Boyd went down swinging. As he stepped to the plate in the final inning, it was his fourth and last time to hit the ball out of the park. He carefully went through the preparations he had always made before facing the pitcher. Hearing the crowd cheer in anticipation, he knocked the mud from his cleats, removed his cap, and pressed his hair down. This time, surely, God's power hitter would knock the ball so far out of the park, no one would ever find it.

Boyd thought a quick, fervent prayer and took his stance. His bat was poised and ready.

"Ball one!" shouted the umpire. Boyd swallowed hard. Not again, he thought. Please, God, don't let me down, he prayed.

"Ball two!"

The next two pitches were strikes, followed by a third ball. If Boyd struck out with the next pitch, the game would end, and his team would have lost. If he hit the ball over the wall, the score would be tied.

The ball came twisting in. Boyd swung. The game was over. The Cavemen had lost.

After the game the scout from the Yankees, along with several others, surrounded the left-handed pitcher. None of them spoke to Boyd.

Boyd was never the same after that day. He stopped going to church with his mother. And though he never said so, it seemed that he stopped praying as well.

The next year Boyd played semi pro ball for the Rooster Creek team and led them to the championship of the Industrial League. He almost seemed like his old self.

In the spring the Chicago Cubs organization invited him to their tryouts. However, just before he was to attend training camp, he injured his knee and lost the opportunity to participate. The next year he played again on the local team and did well, but his speed had diminished and his hitting was no longer spectacular.

Discouraged, Boyd quit the team and never played or even talked about baseball again. He told his father, who was dying of cancer, never to call him Babe again. At the funeral Boyd sat silently as he thought how he had let this good man down. He felt the weight of his failure and had no doubt that the town's people saw him the same way. After that day, he withdrew into himself and locked his heart against all his tender feelings, becoming a negative and bitter man. Soon all the townspeople had learned that no one had better call Boyd Bush "The Babe" again.

During his years playing on the local team, Boyd had married his high school sweetheart, Katie Jones, and had taken a job on the small Rooster Creek police force. The year after he quit playing baseball, a baby boy was born to the young couple. On the morning of the birth, one of the nurses went from room to room in the little local hospital to tell everyone there that she had seen Boyd Bush smile. Many doubted her words.

According to Katie, little Sonny was the spitting image of Boyd, and people thought that the child's birth had caused the tough policeman to be a little less stinging in his treatment of law breakers and a bit more civil to the local citizens.

Since Boyd no longer went to church he felt that there was no need for the baby to ever go there. After a few months Bishop Tattersall appeared at the Bush home to ask Boyd when he wanted to have the baby blessed at church. Boyd replied coldly, "I don't think things like prayers and blessings make much difference in how things turn out."

Nevertheless, the bishop's reply was cordial as he said, "It's up to you but if you change your mind, let me know."

After the bishop had departed, Katie pled for Boyd to arrange to have the baby blessed. However, Boyd didn't have much talent for ever changing his mind.

From then on, Boyd lived for the times he could be with his smiling, curly-haired son.

Six years later, Boyd's mother died. The only bright moment in his heartbreaking grieving was when he learned that he had inherited her violin. A week later, as he sat alone in his front room thinking of his mother, he went to the closet and gently took the violin in his hands. Sitting in his easy chair, he caressed the instrument in his hands, recalling how his mother had tried to get him to learn to play it.

"How different it would have been if only I had spent my time doing that," he thought, and then there came into his heart a dream for Sonny. He imagined his young son becoming a concert violinist.

The next week he arranged for lessons with a violin teacher over in Lehi City, and for the next few years he insisted that Sonny take lessons and spend hours every week practicing.

"Sonny needs to have other interests as well," Katie insisted. "He should be outside playing with the other children. He could even be playing baseball."

But whenever she said something like this, Boyd grew silent. His mind was set and he could see no reason to discuss it. His son was not going to go through what he had gone through. Baseball and God had ruined his life. That would not happen to his child.

One day in December 1958, Boyd came home from his day shift on the police force and sat on the worn couch reading the *Deseret News*. Sonny, who had been in the backyard playing, came running inside when he saw his father. Waving a paper in his hand, he shouted, "Look, Daddy! I wrote a letter to Santa."

Boyd looked up at his son and smiled. "What did you say to him?" he asked, drawing his son beside him on the couch.

Sonny's blue eyes sparkled as he looked at his father. "I told him I wanted a ball and bat!"

Boyd lifted his son onto his lap, held him tightly, and said nothing.

Sonny looked up at him anxiously. "He'll bring me a ball and bat, won't he, Daddy?"

But Boyd didn't answer. As he took the letter and read it, his mind went back to his younger days of playing with his baseball, hour after hour. All he had ever wanted for Christmas was a new mitt or bat. For a moment he forgot the pain and a slight smile lifted the corners of his mouth. Then the memories of those later, painful years landed heavily on his heart. Although Boyd wanted to agree with his son's request, he just couldn't. There would be no ball in the house this year or ever. This year's gifts would be something constructive like tinker toys, and maybe some books on science and music—things that would be part of his son's success, not his failure.

Two nights before Christmas, Boyd walked through the brightly decorated business district of Rooster Creek. As he moved along he checked the safety of each business place. Soon he was at the steps that led down to what was known as "Sig Ronson's Pool Hall." Sig's father, who was the richest man in town, had bought the pool hall so that his forty-year-old son would have some kind of work to do. Mentally challenged and childlike, Sig didn't exactly "manage" the pool hall; he wasn't really up to that. However, he could collect the money and do simple tasks that needed to be done. He was friendly and kept the pool hall meticulously clean.

Most of the townfolks liked Sig. No one in Rooster Creek seemed to enjoy life as much as Sig did. His face held a perpetual grin. He seldom spoke without laughing. Much to the dismay of his father, he gave most of his money to people that he felt needed it more than he did. He was, in a strange way, one of the best known and most loved men in town. He was known as the man who started to celebrate Christmas the day after Halloween.

Boyd liked Sig and went to the pool hall as often as duty would allow. Now he walked down the stairs and entered the large room. There, in addition to the four pool tables, he saw a brightly decorated Christmas tree in the corner closest to the stairs. Against each of the four walls leaned a large cardboard cutout figure of Santa Claus. Looking at these, Boyd removed his police hat and ran his hand through his prematurely graying hair.

"Hello, Officer Bush, how are you doing?" asked Sig in a loud voice like an excited child. He seemed as happy to see Boyd as if Boyd were his best friend in the whole town.

Boyd wanted to smile as he looked upon the grinning childlike face. But smiling wasn't his style and when he replied, both his expression and his voice were stern. "Sig," he said, "why in the world have you got those Santa Claus pictures down here? This is a pool hall. No kids ever come in here. Nobody down here cares a lick about Santa Claus."

Sig just grinned. He was used to Boyd's pessimism. "I sent away for those," he explained happily. "I saved my money all summer to get them. Doesn't it make you happy just looking at them?"

Boyd shook his head in mild disgust and looked around the room once more before walking out the door. "Good-bye, Officer Bush!" shouted Sig. "Merry Christmas!"

Boyd couldn't figure out why seeing Sig always made him feel happier inside although he pretended it didn't. Right now he had a feeling that made him want to go shopping. He walked down the block and entered the J.C. Penney store. Several of the locals called out, "Hello," and "How ya doin'?" but he didn't look their way. He made a beeline to the back where the toys were, pausing a moment at the sports equipment. Without intending to, he picked up a baseball and held it in his right hand. Sonny's voice came back to him: "Look, Daddy! I wrote a letter to Santa. I told him I wanted a ball and bat."

The ball felt good in his hand. He threw it up a foot or two and caught it. Holding it tightly in his hand, Boyd stared at it.

"Maybe..." He stood there a moment, lost in thought. Then he shook his head, clearing away the memories. Slowly, he put the ball back and looked around him. He took a few steps and saw what he wanted. It was a large box of tinker toys. Picking it up, he muttered to himself, "This is the kind of toy a child needs." Next he walked over to the books. Instead of just buying three, he added a fourth one that he hadn't planned on at all. Then, without really intending to, he purchased some Lincoln Logs. He loved his son more than he had ever loved anyone or anything. He hoped these gifts would show that.

Chapter 2

Christmas Eve

On Christmas Eve Officer Bush left his home on Third Street, and because he had plenty of time, he decided to walk to work, leaving the car for Katie. The two other policemen, who each had several children, wanted to spend the evening with their families, and Boyd was happy to take the Christmas Eve shift so he could be home on Christmas Day to see Sonny open his presents.

After getting to the station he climbed into the 1958 Ford police car and drove the short distance to the Main Street, where he would wait and watch. Not much was happening in the little country town of Rooster Creek on Christmas Eve as Boyd parked the car just south of the People State Bank. He pulled a thick blanket up across his shoulders to keep him warm as he sat and contemplated the quiet town.

He thought of Christmases past, and of Sonny, and his wife, Katie. Suddenly the quiet was shattered by the sound of a truck's motor. The noise of the engine, obviously missing a muffler, jolted Boyd back to his full senses. He could hardly believe his eyes when an old delivery truck passed him, clearly moving faster than the twenty-five mile per hour speed limit. Sitting up and quickly starting the engine, Boyd started after the truck, which had a large box-like bed on the back. It was so high, in fact, that it caught and tore down one of the low-hanging strands of Christmas lights strung across Main Street. Boyd knew how proud Mayor Devey was with his eighty-seven ropes of Christmas lights and knew he would be outraged at this wanton destruction. The proud city leader had made certain that Rooster Creek had twice as many strands of lights as could be seen on the main street of nearby Lehi City.

Boyd had turned on his flashing lights, but for the first block of the chase he did not sound the siren, not wanting to disturb the quiet of Christmas Eve. But the truck apparently hadn't seen his flashing lights because it wasn't pulling over. If anything, it seemed to be going even faster. Boyd reluctantly flipped on the siren and after another block the truck finally pulled over just before Dave Greenwood's service station.

Boyd had a hard time keeping his anger under control as he climbed out of his car and walked toward the truck. He wondered who would speed through Rooster Creek, a city in which each and every citizen took pride in obeying the law to the very letter. He was amazed when he saw the driver was Sig Ronson, the childlike manager of the pool hall.

"Sig?" Boyd said in disbelief. "What do you think you're doing speeding through town like you was Roy Griffin driving the fire engine? This stupid truck is so big it tore down the most colorful string of lights in this whole county."

Sig's normally cheerful face was almost white with fear. "Don't arrest me, please," he begged. "I have a lot I have to do tonight."

Boyd couldn't imagine what Sig was doing out on Christmas Eve and where he had got a truck. He knew for a fact that Sig didn't have a driver's license. Despite Sig's protests, Boyd led him to the police car and opened the door. As if realizing that he had no choice, Sig sat down on the front seat without a word. Boyd made a U-turn and headed back to the center of town.

At the police station, Boyd indicated that Sig should take a seat beside the old wooden desk. "Where did you get that truck, Sig?" Boyd asked. Sig looked away and did not reply.

"Did you steal it?"

Sig, whose hands were shaking, was silent.

Boyd stared at him, wondering what had happened to the normally cheerful Sig, who had never given anyone any trouble before this. "You know stealing is wrong, Sig," he said. "I'm afraid I'm going to have to lock you up until we can get to the bottom of this."

Sig's eyes grew wide. "Oh, no! Please don't do that. I'll come in tomorrow and you can keep me here for a week, but not tonight."

Boyd raised his eyebrows. "You should have thought of that before you drove down Main Street like it was the Salt Flats," he said dryly.

With that Boyd took Sig by the arm and led him to the back of the station, to the only cell that the jail had. He opened a closet and pulled out two blankets, tossed them on the bed, closed the door behind Sig, and turned the key. Then he tugged at the door to make certain it was locked.

Soon Boyd was back in his car across from the bank. He felt bad that he had put a normally law-abiding citizen in jail on Christmas Eve, but what else could he have done?

A few minutes later Boyd caught a movement along the side of the road. To his surprise he saw the figure of a man hurrying from shadow to shadow down the street toward the bank. Boyd watched, his eyes narrowed as the man ran by Cook's Ice Cream store and passed the mortuary. By the time Boyd started his car and moved onto the street, the man was nearly to Dave Greenwood's service station. For a second time that night, the siren wailed as Boyd sped along the road. Skidding to a stop in front of the old truck, he saw that the man had climbed inside and started the engine.

Boyd almost slipped in the snow as he jumped from the car and ran to the truck. Once again, he found Sig sitting there with both hands clutching the steering wheel. Sig gave Boyd a brief terrified glance as he began to pull away, but Boyd jumped on the running board and held on.

"Stop right now!" he yelled.

Sig looked at him wildly and apparently saw the determination on Boyd's face, because he gave a sigh and began to apply the brake.

When the truck had stopped, Boyd demanded, "How did you get out of jail, Sig?"

Sig's face was resigned. "I used my key," he said.

"What key?" Boyd asked suspiciously.

"The key that unlocks everything," Sig whispered, not looking at Boyd.

Boyd was baffled. "What are you talking about? There isn't any such key."

Sig looked at him. "There is tonight," he said as he pulled a shining key from his pocket and held it out for Boyd to see.

Boyd stared at the key. "Well, now," he said thoughtfully, "if that key will unlock everything, then let's just use it on the lock on the back door of this big old delivery truck and see what you got in there."

Sig looked horrified. "Oh don't make me do that, Boyd! I can't do that."

Boyd was implacable. "C'mon now," he said sternly.

His reluctance clear on his face, Sig stepped down from the truck's cabin and went around to the back of the truck where he opened the lock. The two doors flew wide open. As Boyd flashed his long, six-battery flashlight inside, his mouth fell open in surprise. The truck was crammed full of toys. Boyd could see small bikes, teddy bears, balls, Barbie Dolls, doctor sets, and dozens of other toys.

Dumbfounded, he managed to ask, "Where did you get all that stuff?"

Sig seemed resigned to telling the truth. "Out by the Saratoga road bridge," he said.

Boyd knew the area well and picturing that desolate place, replied, "There's no store there. Nothing but open fields and trees and the Jordan River."

Sig shook his head. "Yes there is. It's the distribution center for Lehi, Rooster Creek, and Pleasant Grove."

Boyd had never heard of such a thing. "Distribution center?"

Sig was looking down at his feet. In a low voice, he said, "It's too much for him to take them to the individual houses so he drops them off there, and we pick them up and deliver them."

Still shining his flashlight on the toys, Boyd looked over at Sig. "What are you talking about?" he demanded.

Sig looked up. "I can't tell you. I promised never to tell. That's how I got the job."

"What job?" Boyd was torn between impatience and curiosity.

"Getting the toys to where they are supposed to go," Sig mumbled.

Boyd was stymied. He had never encountered anything like this. In the past ten years, he had solved a bank robbery, the theft of a diamond ring at Garth Reid's jewelry store by a guy who wanted to get married but had no money, and several other cases, but he had encountered nothing like this before. Although he doubted that Sig had taken part in any serious crime, he knew something was wrong. "This truck could be stolen and it's a cinch that these toys are," he said, mostly to see what Sig would say.

"I'm not a thief! I'd never steal nothing," Sig said indignantly. "This truck belongs to the Mary Pulley turkey farm. They use it to haul feed and to take their turkeys down to the processing plant. They know I got it."

"Do they know you haven't got a driver's license?" Boyd asked.

"They don't care," Sig insisted. "Before she died, Mary made arrangements for me to use the truck on Christmas Eve. She was part of the plan. You know how much she loved kids. She gave out candy up at her place every night when they came to see the lights on her trees. She couldn't stand to see a kid unhappy."

Boyd was silent, his mind caught on the words, "She was part of the plan." He hardly heard Sig's next words.

"Mary was a real believer in Christmas," Sig was saying. He described how he had been in Chipman's Department store looking at the candy when Mary had seen him. "Hi, Sigmond," she had said and then she had asked him what he believed in.

"She always called me Sigmond," Sig added. "Anyway, I told her about my religion and praying and that. She asked me what I believe about Christmas. I told her it was the birthday of Jesus. Then she said, 'Do you know how toys get into all the houses on Christmas Eve?' I didn't want to tell her the truth so I said that parents put them there. She smiled and said, 'You don't really believe that, do you, Sigmond?' I couldn't lie to a lady like that. I had to tell her truth about what I really believe. And then she said, 'Sigmond, you are just the one I need to help me.'"

By now Boyd was listening to Sig and trying to make sense of his words. But Sig wasn't done with his story yet.

Sig went on to tell how Mary had asked him the following year to help her put the lights on the trees at her house. While he was there she showed him her truck and taught him how to drive it. Then on Christmas Eve she took Sig out to the Saratoga road bridge.

Sig sighed happily, remembering. "I saw three big piles of toys. I'd never seen so many toys. There was a pile there with a sign saying 'Rooster Creek' and the words, 'Merry Christmas.'"

The two of them had loaded up the toys and headed into town. Mary had told Sig that what they were doing was a pilot program that the officials "up North" wanted to try out to see if it could help solve the problem of one man trying to get to all the houses in one night. That had been ten years ago, and Mary and Sig had been doing it every year since then. They always used back roads so nobody ever saw them, but when Mary became sick, Sig went on his own. The next year, just before Mary died, she called Sig to her bedside and told him a secret. It was his responsibility to keep up the work and she even gave him a special key. She said it would fit the truck and all the doors in Rooster Creek.

Boyd had said nothing all this time. He had never heard anything so incredible. Sig waited, and then getting no response from Boyd, he said, "I got to get going. I promise I'll come back after I get through and you can lock me up for a year. No other adult in town can do this. They don't believe, and if you don't believe then none of this can happen."

Boyd found his voice at last. "Who are those toys for?"

"They're for the kids who ordered them," Sig said.

At last Boyd thought he understood. The kids had ordered the toys. "You mean from the Montgomery Ward catalog?" he said.

But Sig shook his head wildly. "No! Not that way. Parents order that kind of stuff. These are from the orders sent to . . . don't make me say it, Boyd. If you do, then it won't work."

Boyd stared at him, trying to understand. "Let me get this straight. Is this the stuff that parents bought for their kids and now has been delivered out there at the bridge?"

"No! Course not!" Sig said, growing exasperated. "What the parents get for the kids is for kids who know that the parents give them Christmas stuff. None of this stuff is for them. A kid don't have to believe to get stuff like that."

Sig's words didn't make sense. "You mean the parents don't have anything to do with this?" Boyd asked. "You do all this on your own? Where do you get the money?"

Sig looked at Boyd and Boyd could almost swear he saw pity in Sig's eyes. "This stuff doesn't have anything to do with money.

It can't be bought with money."

"Then how do you get it?" Boyd insisted on knowing.

"It's bought with wishes," Sig said softly. "Little kid wishes."

Then, as if speaking of the children had reminded him of his mission, Sig's voice became more urgent. "Kids get up really early so I only have a couple hours left. You got to let me go. Please! Let me go!"

Although Boyd didn't understand everything Sig said, he understood part of it at least. "You going to deliver those toys to all the kids?" he asked.

"To some of them," Sig replied.

"Which ones?"

"The ones who still believe."

The night was quiet as the two men stood there, their words hanging between them. At last Boyd said quietly, "If you mean who I think you mean, I thought he did his own work."

Sig seemed to understand that he could speak honestly at last. "He used to," he said, "but the world is so big now. And so many people don't even have chimneys. So he has this pilot program to see if it will work. He still goes to most houses but he can't get to them all. So he has these distribution centers. He needs our help."

Boyd understood that he could detain Sig no longer. "Since you don't have a license, I'd feel better if I followed you."

Sig's eyes nearly popped from his head. "Oh no!" he cried. "You can't follow me. This isn't police work. This is the work of . . . well, anyway, you can't follow me or this will be the saddest Christmas Rooster Creek has ever known."

Boyd stood there, undecided. Then, against his better judgment he told Sig to get on his way. As the old truck engine started and rumbled away, he walked back to his car, deep in thought. He could see that Sig was again speeding, but he knew now was not the time to make an arrest.

🎄 Chapter 3 🎄

Christmas Day

A sudden noise startled Boyd and automatically he reached for his gun.

"Hey, hold on!" The voice sounded familiar. "It's just me. I thought you might be ready to get home and celebrate Christmas with your family."

Boyd looked around him. He was sitting in the police car, blanket around his shoulders. Beyond the car he saw a covering of snow everywhere. He also felt a chilly breeze and realized that Officer TJ Turner was standing outside the open car door. Boyd felt a bit embarrassed when he realized that he had been sleeping on the job. He had never done that before.

But TJ didn't seem bothered by it. "You must have had a quiet night. I guess the big snowstorm kept everybody off the streets. I can see the car hasn't moved all night. It's so deep out there I'm not sure I can get her out without doing some shoveling."

Boyd was surprised to see the snow. It must have started sometime after he let Sig go. He wondered vaguely how Sig had managed to get around in the big delivery truck last night... or was it this morning?

As he got out of the car, he remembered something. Turning to TJ, he said, "I'll get somebody up here to fix that strand of lights so the mayor won't get all bent out of shape."

TJ looked up and down along the street, and then asked, "What strand of lights?"

"A truck knocked it down last night," Boyd said, looking around trying to find the fallen lights.

TJ laughed. "Somebody must have put it back up because I don't see it now." He picked up his snow shovel and started digging around the wheels of the car, then paused, seeing that Boyd was still standing there, staring at the lights. "You better get home and see the lump of coal that Santa brought you," he added, jokingly.

Boyd didn't respond, not appreciating TJ's humor. Instead he said, "I'll just walk by the station before I head on home."

At the station, Boyd walked directly to the cell where he had escorted Sig the night before. He jerked on the door and found it locked. The cell was empty and had a deserted look, as if no one had been there in a long time. The blankets that Boyd had placed on the bed were nowhere in sight.

When he reached home, even before he stepped onto the front porch, Boyd could hear Sonny's voice and laughter. He opened the door and met the bright eyes of his son, who was standing in the middle of the front room.

"Dad, look what Santa brought me," he shouted. In one hand he held a baseball and in the other a bat.

Boyd stopped in his tracks, his smile fading. What had Katie done? She knew how he felt about baseball.

Sonny handed the ball to his father, then backed up a few feet, and said, "Pitch it to me, Daddy." The boy stood poised with the bat on his shoulder and looked at Boyd expectantly, "C'mon, throw it to me!" he begged.

Boyd couldn't resist his son's pleas, and after a dramatic windup that left Sonny giggling, he tossed a gentle, underhanded pitch towards his son. The boy swung the bat with great gusto, and the ball sailed in a line drive across the room, shattering the front room window. Katie, hearing the sound of breaking glass, came running in from the kitchen. Boyd and the boy stared at each other in wonder. After a long silence, Boyd smiled and looked at Katie and said, "The boy is a natural!" Enthusiasm and pride rang in his voice.

After Boyd had patched the window, the family sat down to breakfast. As they ate their Rice Krispies, Sonny clutched the ball in his left hand and held the bat across his lap. "After we eat, can we go outside and play some more?" he asked his father.

Boyd smiled. "We'll see." Reaching over, he took his wife's hand and said softly, "I admit I was a little upset when Sonny came running up with a baseball and bat in his hands. But now I see you were right. Thanks for getting him the ball and bat. I should have done that a long time ago."

Katie looked at him in surprise. "Don't blame me. I didn't get those for him. I know how you feel. I wasn't about to make you mad, especially on Christmas Day."

"But it's okay, I'm not mad at you," Boyd said. "I'm glad you did it."

"But I didn't," Katie repeated. "I thought you had. When I came downstairs this morning and saw the package, I figured you had left it for Sonny. Then, when I saw what was inside, I realized you must have changed your mind."

Boyd stared at his wife. He prided himself on his ability to discern when people were telling the truth, and Katie's face was without guile.

"Let me see if I understand," he said. "You really didn't get those for him?" He nodded his head toward Sonny, who still clutched his ball and bat.

"No I didn't." She looked at him, searching his face for signs of teasing. "But I don't mind if you did. You don't have to apologize for changing your mind."

"But I didn't . . ." Boyd began then turned to Sonny, who had been listening and now decided it was time to speak up.

"Santa brought them. You remember the letter I wrote to him. He brought them."

Boyd didn't say anything as he finished eating. He had long taught others to lock their doors. Had he forgotten to lock his own? Or . . .

He shook his head in bewilderment, then decided not to let his questions get in the way of enjoying the day. He jumped to his feet, pulled Katie into his arms, held her close, and whirled her around. "Merry Christmas!" he said, only a little breathless when he set her down.

Laughing, she replied, "What in the world? You haven't done that since our high school Christmas ball when we were elected Mr. and Mrs. Santa."

Boyd laughed along with her. He had completely forgotten that night. How long ago it seemed, and yet, he felt just as happy right now as he did then.

"Get your coat on, Sonny," he called. "The snow is already starting to melt so let's go on outside. This game has been put off far too long. It's time to play ball."

As he hurried toward the door, Boyd looked back at Katie. "I tell you, honey," he said happily, "that kid is a natural."

With every pitch to his son, Boyd could almost feel his heart softening. As he thought about all that had happened in the last twelve hours, he thought maybe Sig had been right. On the third pitch Sonny hit the ball over the outstretched arm of his laughing father. Running though the snow to get the ball, Boyd couldn't help smiling.

"Apparently Sig's key can open more than doors," he thought as he reached down and picked up the ball. "Maybe next Christmas Eve I can even help him. Right now I sure do feel qualified."

⚶ Chapter 4 ⚶

The Christmas City

After that Christmas, Boyd Bush was happier than he had been since he had been a boy. During the month of January, he thought many times of his Christmas Eve experience although he wasn't entirely sure what had happened. He asked himself repeatedly, "Could a dream be that real?"

By February he finally decided that what he had experienced had been a dream. Despite what Katie had said, he was sure that she had bought the ball and bat for Sonny. He reasoned, "It was the right thing to do and she always does the right thing."

But still he wondered. He wondered about Sig, determined to keep a close watch on him next Christmas Eve. During his police rounds he drove past Mary Pulley's place, looking for anything that might provide some kind of clue. As he passed the northeast corner of her property, he saw an old, apparently abandoned truck and quickly pulled over to the curb. When he walked over to the barbed wire fence to have a better look, he could see that the hood was up and someone had removed the engine. The tires were all flat.

Climbing back into his car, he found himself humming and soon began to sing. "Jolly Old Saint Nicholas, lean your ear this way..." Lately he had discovered that he liked to sing songs like that when he was alone in the police car.

Although Christmas was still many months away, Boyd's head and heart were full of Christmas. One day a driver from out of town sped along Main Street going at least ten miles over the limit, and Boyd pulled him over. He walked to the car, leaned down toward the window, and greeted the embarrassed driver, "Merry Christmas, my dear friend." Giving the man a ticket, he added, "I give you the love of this whole city."

Startled, the man gave a bewildered smile. "Uh, why, thank you, Officer," he stammered.

Boyd, who liked to be called "Officer," sat in his car and felt happy he had administered justice, but had done so in a friendly, loving, and merciful manner. Now he started thinking, "How can I get everyone to feel about Christmas the way that I do?"

Then like a flash of lightning it came to him! He would make Rooster Creek the Christmas City. For the next week he thought of nothing else. He formulated a plan. Three days later he went to the city council meeting, where he proposed to Mayor Devey and the council members that he felt Rooster Creek should become known as "The Christmas City." He had such good will and enthusiasm that the city council was quite taken by his idea. After all, they reasoned, "If Lehi can be the Cowboy City, Rooster Creek needs to be some kind of city."

Boyd then proposed that the welcome signs at both ends of town should not only say "Welcome to Rooster Creek," but should also say, "The Christmas City." Mayor Devey about fell out of his chair he was so excited.

Heinz Leonhardt, a member of the council, was the only one to oppose the idea, but the mayor called him a "Scrooge" and the others voted him down. Boyd, now on a roll, further suggested that the city motto be "the city where Christmas is celebrated 365 days of the year."

The council, led by the mayor, applauded wildly at this idea. Ruth Gaisford, the reporter for the Citizen, the local newspaper, frantically took notes. Not a word of these ideas would escape her Thursday article.

A week later when the locals read the headlines, "Rooster Creek to Become the Christmas City," Boyd Bush found himself in the unusual position of being the most popular man in town. Sign painters were soon at work adding "The Christmas City" to the city signs. Boyd persuaded the other two police officers to greet every person they pulled over with the words "Merry Christmas." Charlie Carson and two others drove all the way from Cedar Fort just to get a ticket in Rooster Creek because of the spirit of the police officers. It was a glorious thing to be a Rooster Creeker in those days when every person had the Christmas spirit every day.

But Boyd didn't stop there. In March he proposed a plan where Rooster Creek would be the home of the "Santa Claus helpers for the whole world." Boyd's mission was to have everyone catch the spirit of Santa Claus as deeply as he had caught it.

Committees were organized to begin to collect money and make toys for less fortunate children. Christmas was indeed coming alive in Rooster Creek and it was only April 6th.

Boyd now attended each city council meeting. At the May 14th meeting his name was, as usual, at the top of the agenda. He proposed that a big celebration be held in Rooster Creek at Christmas time—on Christmas Day itself. The council agreed and voted unanimously to appoint Boyd as the chairman. For the first time in many years people could see Boyd's eyes glistening with tears as he spoke to them. In an emotional voice he asked, "Could we all sing what I hope can be our new city song, 'Santa Claus Is Coming to Town'?" They all rose to their feet and sang with great gusto the few words of the song that they could remember. It was a touching moment for each of them—even Heinz had his hanky in hand. As Boyd departed the mayor shouted, "Hey, Boyd, Merry Christmas!" Boyd had never been happier.

That week Boyd visited the local pool hall to see Sig Ronson, a man he now looked upon as his hero. He wanted to find out where Sig had got his cardboard cutouts of Santa Claus. Next,

Boyd appointed a committee to start raising money to buy the cardboard cutouts of Santa for every business in the community. He asked the businesses to pay half the cost. In June the cardboard cutouts arrived. Every business had a cardboard cutout of Santa Claus near the front entry. People came from as far away as Lindon to see the Christmas City that was plumb full of Santa Clauses.

Next, Boyd approached KJ Bird, the famous local band leader and asked if his band would learn to play every song there was about Santa Claus. This would prepare them to play Santa Claus songs nonstop all the way from the Latona Dance Hall to Dave Greenwood's service station. KJ, who loved the colors red and white, eagerly agreed.

Boyd was on fire with Christmas. He convinced the mayor that the town should hang up its Christmas lights in July. They did so and hung even more than ever before. Fund-raisers were set up to help to pay for those lights, since the mayor said he couldn't pay for them out of the city budget. When it was decided to cancel the Fourth of July fireworks to help cover the cost, everyone was supportive except for Heinz Leonhardt. But since he didn't want to be labeled "Scrooge," he kept his thoughts to himself.

The name of Boyd Bush was now on the lips of everybody in the town. And if Boyd was the happiest, most popular man in town, Sig Ronson was second happiest, seeing all the cardboard cutouts of Santa Claus all over town—although he wondered what had happened to Boyd, who had scoffed at the cardboard cutouts the first time he saw them.

As plans were made for the biggest celebration of all, which would be held on Christmas Day, Boyd could scarcely sleep at night. He could picture in his mind the Rooster Creek band marching down Main Street playing, "Here Comes Santa Claus." This vision served to strengthen his resolve as he went door-to-door getting every businessman to commit to building a float for the parade. Each float was to honor Santa in some unique way.

The *Deseret News* published a big article about Rooster Creek becoming "The Christmas City" and Boyd's picture was there on the front page of the center section. The article was picked up by the *Associated Press* and was soon published in newspapers all over the country. Other cities wanted to know how they could become like Rooster Creek and have the Christmas spirit 365 days a year.

By August the whole community was ablaze with Christmas lights and the Christmas spirit. People were making toys and raising money to send to far-off lands so that everyone could have a wonderful Christmas. Boyd spoke to the Lions Club, the Rotary Club, The Veterans of Foreign Wars, The TOPS Club, the elementary School, and the high school, helping to generate enthusiasm for the big celebration on Christmas Day.

Finally, it was November. Boyd's plans were all coming together.

Then one night, the stake president, who was the leader of the area churches, was looking through the local newspaper. As he read an article about the plans for the Christmas celebration, a smile crossed his face. "What a wonderful thing is happening," he thought as he looked at his calendar to make sure that he could do his part to help. He then noticed for the first time that this year Christmas was going to fall on Sunday.

Nevertheless, he didn't anticipate any difficulty changing the celebration to Christmas Eve, the day before Christmas. In fact, he thought it might even work out better, so that families could be home together on Christmas.

He called Mayor Devey to talk it over with him. The mayor was in complete agreement with him. "Oh, President Jensen, I'm sure that shouldn't be any problem. Let's change it to Saturday."

Unfortunately, the two leaders failed to communicate this change to Boyd. The next week an announcement appeared in The Citizen that the celebration had been changed to Saturday—

the day before Christmas.

Boyd learned of the change from Lisha Boley at the local meat market. At first he was shocked. Then he became angry. How dare they change the day of his celebration?

He charged down to the City Hall and demanded to see the mayor. Such was his standing that he was admitted at once although Louise Mitchell, the mayor's secretary, thought she had never seen him looking so red faced and glowering. Inside the mayor's office, Boyd stood over the startled city leader and demanded to know what was going on. The mayor asked him to be seated and said, "Yes, well, we're going to have the celebration on Christmas Eve. We think that will be even better because it will allow the people to go to church and then stay at home on Christmas with their families. That way they can celebrate the real meaning of Christmas."

Boyd, who had just sat down, stood up again and looked down at the mayor. "What do you mean 'the real meaning of Christmas'? The town celebration and the parade is what Christmas is all about. We've got to have that parade on Christmas Day. KJ Bird is ready to play and the floats are being made. The celebration can't happen on Saturday—it has to happen on Sunday. Sunday is Christmas Day and we are the Christmas City. We are not the Christmas Eve City. It has to be on Sunday!"

With this Boyd stormed out of the city hall building. As he did, Louise Mitchell called out, "Hey, Boyd, Merry Christmas," but Boyd did not reply.

The town's people, who had grown accustomed to friendly greetings from the man they considered their friendliest policeman, found that he was back to his old grumpy self, and they wondered what was wrong. When he arrived home he was so upset that he would hardly speak to Katie. He even scolded Sonny for not practicing the violin that day.

The mayor immediately called the stake president and told

him what had happened. President Jensen was shocked at Boyd's attitude but said only, "We've got to have this celebration on Saturday. We're not going to violate the Sabbath Day by having a parade." Mayor Devey, who was also a faithful member of the church, said that he agreed. He would apologize to Boyd for not talking to him before making the change. He thought he could then talk some sense into Boyd after he had calmed down.

But Boyd didn't calm down. He went to every businessman in town telling each one what had happened. He got many of them to sign a petition saying that they felt the parade should be on Sunday, not Saturday.

The stake president and the mayor arranged a meeting with Boyd and held it at the city hall building since Boyd said he would never come to any meeting at the church. As Boyd entered the stake president's office, President Jensen reached out to shake his hand but Boyd looked the other way.

As they all took their seats, Boyd appeared outwardly calm. He quietly but firmly explained his reasons why he felt the celebration should be on Sunday and not Saturday. He felt confident that he could convince the leaders he was right. The two other men listened patiently, but when Boyd had finished, the mayor said simply, "Boyd, we can't have this on Sunday. That's the Sabbath Day."

Boyd's voice rose as he blurted out, "It's also Christmas Day. Christmas Day is the day this town has been looking forward to all year. They have Sunday every week. I've never seen so much excitement in this town. Good will is in every home and on every street corner. That is true religion. If you want to have a real religious thing on Sunday, it should be the parade and this big celebration."

President Jensen moved forward in his chair and said, "Boyd, we can't violate what this city stands for."

Boyd shook his head. He would have none of that. "This city

stands for good will and helping each other," he said. "People look at those signs when they come into the city. They see that this is a Christmas city, and it changes their hearts."

President Jensen could see that Boyd's mind was set. He tried again to help Boyd see what he was saying. "Boyd, I understand what you are doing. I think it's the most wonderful thing that has ever happened to this town. But we just can't have this on Sunday. We just can't."

Boyd had heard enough. He stood up and moved toward the door, then turned and pointed his finger at the two men. "You just watch!" he said. "You'll see it happen. A lot of people in this town support me in this. So if we don't have your support, that's just fine." With those words Boyd was gone.

For many months Boyd had crusaded for Christmas. Now he spent all his spare time talking to people about moving forward with his original plan. To anyone who would listen, Boyd would say, "Let the city run the city, and the church run the church."

The people became divided. The spirit of Christmas departed from the town. The band continued to practice Christmas songs, even though half of the members refused to play on Sunday. Since the other half agreed to play, Boyd said half a band was all that was needed. When some of the city businesses refused to continue to work on their floats unless the parade was held on Saturday, Boyd told them the parade would go on with or without their floats; the rest of the businesses would be getting their floats ready.

Chapter 5

The Christmas Gift

Christmas was only twenty-one days away when tragedy struck. Katie had made a hamburger loaf and left it in the oven for Boyd and Sonny before walking the few blocks to see her mother, who was sick. Father and son ate their meal quietly, not speaking. Boyd was thinking about what his next move would be to ensure the success of his Christmas plan. As he took his plate and utensils to the sink, he looked out the small window and discovered that it had started snowing so hard he couldn't even see as far as the big pine tree on the north end of his small lot. Seeing that the snow was quickly piling up, he realized he had better hurry down to the station and make sure the snow-plow truck got into action. He also knew there would be more traffic snarls on the streets than one officer could handle.

A sitter was coming over at seven to stay with Sonny, and Boyd saw that it was nearly seven now. Tousling Sonny's hair, he hurried out the door and jumped into his car. The falling snow had covered the back window, but he didn't want to take time to clear it away. He could use his side view mirrors until he got to the station, where he would brush the snow off. He hurriedly began to back the car out of the driveway, but stopped when he felt the back left tire pass over something. When he got out of the car to see what it was, he was horrified to see the small crumpled body lying underneath his car. Sonny had come out to tell his father good-bye but Boyd, in his hurry, hadn't seen him.

In a panic, Boyd pulled the small, limp body toward him. Sonny appeared to be unconscious and blood was coming from his nose. Boyd felt heartsick.

In the dark despair of his grief, he heard a voice ask, "What happened?"

"I backed over him . . . my son," Boyd sobbed. "I didn't take time to clear the snow off my window. Now . . ." His voice broke. "I've killed him."

The man leaned over and touched Sonny's head gently. Then his hand went to Boyd's shoulder and gripped it, bringing Boyd back to his senses. "Your boy is still alive but we have to get him to the hospital fast. You need to calm down and drive."

With that, the man scooped up Sonny's limp and seemingly lifeless body in his arms and hurried around to the other side of the car. Boyd stood up, got in his car, and started the engine. He forced himself to continue backing the car out into the street, then turned the car toward the hospital. As he drove along, Boyd couldn't keep himself from looking over at Sonny's pale face. The man held the small boy close to his chest, and Boyd heard him whisper, "Dear Father, please bless this boy. You know how much it hurt you when your son suffered. You know what Boyd is feeling now. Please keep this boy alive."

At the hospital Boyd jumped out of the car and ran to the other side where the man stood with Sonny cradled in his arms. Boyd reached out for his son and as he did, he looked up into the stranger's face. Their eyes met and for a brief second neither moved. Then the stranger spoke, "Boyd, I know you're hurting but your son is going to be all right. The doctor is in there and he will know what to do. Go!"

Hurrying toward the door, Boyd felt compelled to look back at the stranger who simply smiled and raised his right hand in farewell. Boyd felt a moment of wonder, even peace, before the weight of his son in his arms brought him back to the reason he had come to the hospital in the first place.

Rooster Creek was building a new, modern hospital north of town with an emergency room and all the latest equipment, but until it was finished this antiquated and inadequate hospital would have to do. Just inside the door Boyd saw old Doc Richards, the town's beloved physician, standing by the front desk talking to a nurse. Both of them looked up at the sound of Boyd coming through the door. There was no time to check Sonny in or fill out insurance papers. One look at the limp body in Boyd's arms made that immediately clear to Doc Richards.

Within seconds, Sonny was lying in the small operating room where Doc Richards and his nurse somberly considered the nearly lifeless form. "He's so badly hurt," the doctor said with a frown. "I don't know if…"

"Please, doctor . . ." said Boyd, who had followed them into the operating room, but he could speak no further.

The doctor looked at Boyd, then back at the small, still form lying before him. He shook his head again, "I just don't know." He took a deep breath and turned away to consult with the nurse, then the two returned to the operating table and began to work intently. At one point the doctor told Boyd he should leave the room, but the anxious father did not move.

The good doctor had been practicing for many years in the town of Rooster Creek and he had been so pleased at the thought of a new, modern hospital. If only the new hospital were ready for us, he thought briefly, but he had to work with what he had. More than once he felt he could do no more for the young boy, but then, somehow, he would realize something more that he could do for his patient. His hands moved swiftly as if with a life of their own.

After what seemed many hours, he stepped back from the operating table and wiped his brow with the back of his hand. Looking apologetically at Boyd, the doctor said, "I've done all I can. All we can do now is wait. We just have to give him some time."

The doctor walked over and placed his hand on Boyd's shoulder. "Let's step out into the hall," he said. "The nurses will take him to our critical care room and then we can go in there."

As they walked through the door, Katie appeared at the other end of the hall. She hurried toward them, tears evident on her grief-stricken face. "What happened?" she asked as she reached them.

Boyd bowed his head as he took her hands in his. "Oh Katie, it's all my fault. If only I'd taken the time to clean the snow off the window, but I didn't."

Katie looked up at the doctor, silently pleading for words of hope. The doctor's words were kind but careful, but he didn't want to make promises he couldn't keep. "We don't know what's going to happen. He could be all right or..." He didn't finish. Instead he said, "I'll be back in a little while to check on him."

Seeing the nurses appear in the hallway, he added, "Here they come with him now. You can follow them into the next room."

Watching the small painful breaths of their beloved son, Katie and Boyd had never felt so helpless. It was the hardest moment of their lives. Boyd put his arm around his wife and said softly, "I'm so sorry, Katie. I don't know what we'll do if..." But his worst fears were better left unspoken, so he said nothing else.

As they stood there together, the boy's breathing seemed to become more and more difficult. With each breath, Boyd wondered if the next breath was going to be his son's last.

Finally Katie spoke softly, "Tell me what happened. I mean, after... did you call the ambulance? Or did the neighbors?"

Boyd had to stop and think. Everything had happened so quickly. Finally he said, "Neither. A man came along just after it happened. He held Sonny while I drove us to the hospital."

"A man? Who was it?" Katie asked.

Boyd looked at her blankly. "I don't know," he said.

Katie shook her head in disbelief. "You know everyone in this town, Boyd. How could you not know him?"

Boyd sat, trying to remember, trying to picture the man's face. "He must have been a stranger. He came over right after it happened and told me to calm down and drive. I don't know what I would have done if he hadn't shown up. He sat beside me holding Sonny and I remember..." Boyd looked at Katie in surprise. "He was praying. I heard him. And when we got to the hospital, he said, 'Boyd, Sonny will be all right, I promise you.'"

Katie gave him a peculiar look. "You say he called you Boyd? And he knew Sonny's name? Then you must know him."

Boyd shook his head in bewilderment. "But I didn't... at least, he wasn't at all familiar to me."

Hearing Sonny's ragged breathing, Katie looked over at the small figure and turned back to Boyd. "Maybe we should pray for him," she said softly.

Boyd nodded. "Go ahead, Katie. You know all about prayer. I haven't prayed since..."

Katie reached and took her husband's hand firmly in hers. "No, Boyd. This is the time for you to pray."

Boyd's eyes filled with tears as he bowed his head. Katie stood silently waiting. At last Boyd said, "Dear God, I got no right to ask any special favors. For a long time I figured I could do everything on my own. But there's nothing I can do for..." his voice trembled, "our boy. Please help him, take care of him. Please make him well."

Boyd could no longer speak for his tears. After a few seconds he said again, "Please help him. In the name of your son, Jesus Christ." He then added, "Please take care of my son like you wanted to take care of yours."

Katie reached over and put her arms around him. "I love you" was all she said.

As the minutes and then the hours passed, Sonny did not get any better. The doctor came back and after looking at Sonny carefully said, "I'm sorry, he just isn't looking any better. His pulse is getting more and more faint. If he survives, it will be a miracle."

Boyd and Katie sat by their young son all night. Dr. Richards came back every hour to check Sonny's condition but he could offer few words of hope. Boyd's fatigue brought his emotions to the surface, and as he clung to Katie, he told her of his great love for her. Every so often, he would call softly to his son, "Can you hear me, Sonny? I love you. I love you, my boy. Come back to us."

Boyd thought a thousand thoughts during those long, dark hours. He thought about his mother and father. About the disappointment of the championship game. He remembered the dream that had changed him—the dream with Sig in it. He thought about the ball and bat that had appeared at his house, though Katie protested she had done nothing. Boyd thought about Katie and how much he loved her. He thought about the sign that said, "The Christmas City" and the stranger who had helped him that night. And in between each of these thoughts, he thought of his son. As he did he silently prayed.

Morning finally came and the sunlight filtered through the lace curtains of the east window. The rays filled the room and shone on the boy, now covered from neck to feet with a white sheet. In the glow of the morning sun, Boyd thought the small figure seemed to glow. As he and Katie moved over closer to Sonny, the boy's small chest seemed motionless.

Standing there, it seemed to Boyd that the sun was there to show his young son the way to heaven. Prompted by an unnameable instinct, Boyd whispered softly, "It's all right, Sonny. You can go if you have to. We'll love you forever and someday we will come and find you."

He felt Katie beside him squeeze him tightly, and at that moment, the boy's whole body seemed to shake. His every muscle appeared to tighten and ripple under the sheet. Panic-stricken, Katie ran the short distance to the office and brought the doctor back with her. Though clearly exhausted, Dr. Richards hurried with her into the room. Lowering the sheet, he listened to Sonny's chest, then looked up at them and smiled. "It's amazing. His pulse is actually getting stronger."

Soon Sonny began to breathe more and more naturally. The old doctor tried to speak but couldn't. At last he managed to say, "I can't promise anything, Boyd, but I think he's going to make it."

Boyd felt his heart swell with hope. As he and Katie each took one of Sonny's hands in theirs, the boy opened his eyes slightly and looked at them. "Where have you been?" he murmured sleepily. "I've been looking for you." Then he closed his eyes and slept, breathing deeply and easily.

That day and thereafter young Sonny continued to improve. One day a visiting physician, Dr. Noyes, came with Dr. Richards to look in on the "miracle boy."

When Dr. Richards explained what he had done, Dr. Noyes looked at him in amazement. He had never heard of such procedures. He asked, "How did you know what to do?"

"I just knew I had to do something and it seemed to come into my mind, and my hands just seemed to know what to do."

"Well, however you got the idea, you obviously saved his life," Dr. Noyes said.

Old Doc Richards shook his head. "If I did, I surely didn't do it alone."

Boyd looked at Katie and squeezed her hand and she squeezed back.

Sonny was in the hospital for two weeks and Boyd never left his side. The other officers worked Boyd's shift. Bishop Tatersall came often and President Jensen came to see them twice a day. Boyd was kind of impressed by that. During his first visit, President Jensen told Boyd that all the people in the stake had fasted the day after the accident. The fact that the whole stake had unitedly pled with Heavenly Father that Sonny would be all right touched Boyd deeply. He had vowed that he would never shake hands with the stake president. Now he could not help reaching his hand out. The stake president gripped the grateful father's hand tightly, and tears came to Boyd's eyes.

As the president was leaving, Boyd spoke, "I've been thinking about our Christmas parade. I've been thinking we should probably hold it on Saturday. That way the people can go to church on Sunday, and then they can stay home with their families." As Boyd said the word "families" he became too choked to say anything more.

President Jensen came closer to Boyd and the two men embraced. "Can you forgive me, President Jensen?" Boyd choked out. "Will you let me come back?"

The president could hardly speak as he answered, "If you can forgive me, I want to be right there in church sitting at your side."

Again Boyd took a few minutes to find his voice before he spoke again. "Santa Claus is good for the other days of the week. But Sunday I want to think of things like the stranger who helped me and the other angels in our lives. I want to think of Jesus Christ who knows how to do the things that can't be done by anyone else."

The Christmas parade down the main street of the Christmas City took place on Saturday. Most of the Rooster Creek citizens, including Heinz Leonhardt, said that it was probably the greatest parade ever held on this earth. KJ Bird's full band was there, and every business had a float there.

After the parade, a gentle snow started to fall. The Christmas gifts that people had made for each other were distributed. Everyone agreed that it was undoubtedly the best Christmas the Christmas City had ever had.

Already Boyd was planning on helping the Christmas City organize and produce the best Nativity Christmas pageant ever held anywhere, to have its premier showing the following Christmas. After all, as Boyd told the city council, "No city can be called 'The Christmas City' unless the center of everything is the baby who made Christmas into Christmas."

The next day, on Christmas Day, Boyd Bush and his family went to church and they never missed another meeting again. From that day on he devoted himself to spending the rest of his time, when he wasn't writing out "Merry Christmas" tickets, to helping his city celebrate Christmas 365 days a year.

When the town citizens insisted that Boyd be the grand marshal of the Christmas parade each year, he accepted the duty on one condition. He insisted, though nobody knew why, that Sig sit at his side.

That Thine Alms May Be In Secret

By George Durrant

That thine alms may be in secret: and thy Father which
seeth in secret himself shall reward thee openly.
—Matthew 6:4

Most folks in Steelville were just a little bit afraid of Big Sam Edwards. Sam had lost his job when the steel plant had cut back, and he hadn't been able to find work during the past six months. He was a proud man; and now, with Christmas coming, he made a few telephone calls to important people telling them that he didn't want any "do-gooders" trying to help his family at Christmas. He gruffly warned, "I'll be staying up on Christmas Eve, and if anybody comes around trying to leave anything at the door, somebody's going to get hurt."

On Christmas Eve, when his wife, Kathryn, and his children had gone to their beds, Sam sat in his small front room with a shotgun draped across his lap. He became so weary that around two o'clock he fell asleep.

The next morning when he awoke, there in front of him he saw a whole pile of toys, a large ham, a small Christmas tree, and an open Bible. For a few seconds, he felt a surge of joy. But then he became angry. To himself he muttered, "I warned them, and somebody will pay for poking their nose into my business." Just then the children came into the room. Seeing the toys, they shouted, "Look, Daddy! See what Santa left us!"

Sam jumped from his chair and quickly stepped between the children and the toys. "Don't touch those things!" he shouted.

"This is not our stuff, and somebody is going to pay for sneaking in here and leaving it. That's breaking and entering, and I'm not going to put up with it."

Sam went quickly to the telephone and called his long-time friend Sheriff Walt Durrant. After several rings the sleepy sheriff picked up the phone. Sam blurted out, "Sheriff, you get over here. Somebody broke into my house. I want them arrested." He hung up.

Sam looked over to the corner of the room where his children were standing in a huddle, gazing longingly at the pile of toys. "You kids get back to bed," he said. They didn't move, but fixed yearning eyes on their mother, who stood behind them. She didn't know what to do. During the past few discouraging months, she had more or less given up on helping Sam. If she voiced her thoughts, it always started an argument.

Sam sternly repeated, "I said get back to bed. It's too early for you kids to be up anyway."

The children reluctantly retreated. Kathryn went into the kitchen and started cooking some oatmeal. Breakfast might be the best meal they were going to have that day.

Thirty-five minutes later, Sheriff Walt Durrant knocked on the door. "Come in!" Sam shouted. The sheriff opened the door and said cheerfully, "Merry Christmas." Sam's only reply was a look of disgust.

"Now, what's happened here?" asked the sheriff.

"Somebody broke in last night and left all of this stuff on the floor, and I want them arrested."

"Well, Sam, that looks like pretty good stuff to me. Did they take anything?"

"No, they didn't take nothing, but I'm fed up with all of the do-gooders in this town. I can take care of myself and my family. I don't need help from nobody. Besides, didn't I tell you to keep those meddlers away from here?"

"Were you gone away last night when they did it?"

"No, I was sitting right there in that chair."

"Well, Sam, you know nobody could have come in here without making a big racket."

Sam, more angry than ever, replied, "They might have made a big racket, but I guess I slept right through it."

"I guess you did," the sheriff drawled. "Funny thing is, when I drove down your lane from the road, I could see that nobody else had been down here since the big snow last night."

"Well, somebody drove or walked in here. Now you find out who it was."

"I told you, there's not a track out there. The snow quit falling last night around nine, and nobody has been in here since then."

"Sheriff, there must be some tracks out there."

"Go see for yourself, if you think you're so smart. See if you can see where anybody came in here."

"I'll show you," said Sam. "I don't know why we pay taxes for a blind sheriff like you anyway."

Together the two men went outside. Sam wandered down the lane searching for some tracks other than those left by the sheriff, but there were none.

He returned to where the sheriff stood. "Let's go around the house," he said. "There will be some tracks out back."

Together they circled the house, but all around it the snow was as smooth as a calm lake. Not a mark on it.

Sam, more irritated than ever, shouted, "Somebody's raked over the tracks."

"Nonsense," said the sheriff, "nobody has been here. I don't know where that stuff came from, but I know this—nobody brought it here."

Sam didn't know what else to say or do. The sheriff spoke as kindly as he could. "Look, Sam, I've got Christmas waiting at home. Why don't you just take the stuff and enjoy it. Forget where it came from. Just be grateful."

Sam's voice was choked with emotion as he replied. "Sheriff, I'm not grateful for nothing, except the stuff I provide for my own family."

The sheriff replied, "I know, Sam. But you'll get work soon. Things will get better." He drove away.

Completely mystified by what had happened, Sam came back into the house and sat in his chair. Kathryn spoke softly. "Sam, what does it matter how it got here? It's here."

Sam's only reply was, "I just can't figure out how somebody came here without leaving no tracks."

Little four-year-old Katie, who was standing nearby with the other children, excitedly said, "Daddy, maybe there's some tracks on top of the house."

"I don't think so, honey," Sam replied gently.

Then it hit him like a light. Some troublemaker had actually rented a helicopter and landed on his roof!

A few minutes later Sam propped his old wooden ladder against the side of the house, and to the amazement of Kathryn and the children he almost ran to the top. Up there he looked carefully around. "Nothing," he muttered. Little Katie called up to him, "Are there any reindeer tracks?"

Sam paused and looked down at her and the other children. Then he winked at Kathryn and said with a chuckle, "Yeah, I think I can see some reindeer tracks over by the chimney."

Suddenly Sam had a feeling that he had not had in years. He shouted out, "Well, what are you kids waiting for? Those toys are for you, you know!"

Soon the ham was cooking in the oven. The children were playing with their toys. The miniature Christmas tree was on the table. Unnoticed by his family, Sam picked up the open Bible. A verse was underlined. He softly read: "That thine alms may be in secret: and thy Father which seeth in secret himself shall reward thee openly." Never before or since has more joy been packed into one little house or into one father's heart than there was at that moment.

From then on and through the years everybody in town knew that Sam had changed. During the next thirty-six years almost everyone had been touched by one of Sam's kindnesses. He'd done everything from helping Arnold Conder build a house to being the chief cook at the annual old folks' dinner. On his sixty-eighth birthday he was honored as the city's most generous citizen. Sheriff Durrant, his closest friend, was appointed to present him the plaque.

Sam wasn't much of a public speaker. As he accepted the award, he awkwardly said, "I don't do no more stuff for others than anybody else around this here town. I just wish I could do like Jesus said in the Bible. I wished I could do something good and do it in secret so nobody would ever know."

As the years went by, in almost every conversation he had with Sheriff Durrant he would say, "You remember, don't you, Sheriff—that Christmas when there was no tracks nowhere? If I could do something good for someone and leave no tracks, that would be the merriest Christmas of all for me." The sheriff would smile and say, "Maybe someday, Sam."

All in the community mourned when Sam's wife died. By now the children were all grown up and married, and had moved to larger cities to get work. They and their children visited Sam as often as they could, but most of the time he was alone.

Now it was once again Christmas Eve. Tomorrow Sam's house would be filled with his children, his grandchildren, and even his two-week-old great-grandson. It was a family tradition for all the family to come home on Christmas afternoon. But tonight he was alone. He would have gone to visit some friends but his eyesight was such that he could no longer drive, and his arthritis made walking a lot less than pleasurable.

At about five o'clock the Gentrys had come over to sing Sam a Christmas carol. They were a young family who during the past summer had moved into the old Conder home across the hayfield from Sam. Their two young children, five-year-old Lexie and three-year-old Ben, had taken a special liking to Sam, and he to them. The family made it a point to give Sam a ride to church every Sunday. The children loved him to tell them stories about when he was little. They and their mom, Marinda Gentry, came to visit him often.

This Christmas Eve tears moistened his cheeks as first Lexie and then Ben hugged him and said, "We love you, Grandpa Sam. Merry Christmas." Just before they left to go home he gave Lexie a doll and Ben a ball. He had wanted to make each of them something, but his hands were not now his servants as they had once been.   Sam watched them through his front window as the little family departed down his driveway toward the country road that led the one block to their home. A heavy snowfall had begun.

Sam, who had difficulty in sleeping anyway, had decided to stay up late this night. As he prepared for bed he looked out of the window and saw that the gentle snow had covered all of the fields in the country neighborhood with a soft smooth whiteness. The snow by then had stopped falling. The winter scene reminded him of that mysterious "trackless" night so long ago.

As he let his mind wander in a multitude of memories, he was suddenly jolted back to reality. Looking out across the field toward the Gentry house he saw an orange glow. To his horror he realized that the Gentrys' house was on fire. Hurrying from his chair he scooped up a jacket on his way to the back door. He quickly climbed the wire fence that separated his house from the hayfield. His pains forgotten in his fears for his friends' safety, he hurried toward the burning house. There he found a group of people standing together near the mailbox. The firetruck had just arrived, and the hurrying men were unrolling hoses and exchanging shouted instructions.

No one saw Sam approach, all eyes being on the leaping flames. Mrs. Gentry was screaming, "Bennie is still in there!" The boy's father shouted, "I'll try again!" but two men grabbed him and shouted, "You can't go back! It's no use!" Unnoticed by anyone, Sam ran around and entered through the back door. He couldn't see because of the thick smoke but that didn't matter because he knew the layout of the house, since he had helped build it. Flames were everywhere. He could feel the heat biting against him. The smoke choked his lungs. Suddenly he heard a faint cough. He blindly made his way toward the sound and found little Bennie lying on the floor. He scooped the crying child up in his arms and, running through the flames, made his way to the back door. Once outside he held the boy close to his body and looked heavenward. After coughing violently for several seconds the child began to cry. He placed little Bennie down on the snow and told him to go out front to the mailbox to his mother.

Now for the first time Sam could feel the pain. His lungs seemed to be on fire and his skin felt as though he had been immersed in boiling water. He wanted to be home. Home was where he wanted to die. Without consciously knowing what he was doing, Sam, as if carried by the angels, crossed the snow-covered field, climbed the fence, and staggered into his home.

A fireman found Bennie crying and making his way through the snow. Soon the little boy was in the arms of his mother, who embraced him as she wept with love and gratitude. As she held him, Bennie repeated over and over, "Sam, Sam, Sam." Overwhelmed with emotion, the parents didn't register this, but someone else did. The former Sheriff Durrant, now too old to be a regular lawman, but always a volunteer, stood up straight, and a look of wonder crossed his face. "Sam," he said softly to himself, and he walked back a few yards so that he could see across the field. Just as he did, he saw the light go on in Sam's bedroom window.

The sheriff walked back to where he could watch as Doctor Jones looked at the boy. After just a minute the doctor said to the family, "He looks fine, other than his curly hair is mostly gone. But why don't you drive down to the hospital, and I'll come down and we'll have a good look. Then we'll find a good place for you to stay until the house can be rebuilt."

The sheriff tapped the doctor on the shoulder and said, "You rode out on the firetruck. Why don't you let me give you a lift down to the hospital." As the old sheriff and the doctor pulled out of the Gentry lane, the sheriff said, "Let's just stop in and wish old Sam a Merry Christmas. It will only take a minute."

The doctor replied, "He'd be sleeping, wouldn't he?"

"No, I don't think so," the sheriff replied. "I think he stays too busy to sleep much."

As they pulled down Sam's lane, the sheriff said softly, "No tracks in or out."

"What's that?" asked the doctor.

"Oh, nothing."

The deep new snow on the doorstep was undisturbed. The two men knocked, but there was no response. The door was not locked. The sheriff pushed it open and entered. The doctor said, "Let's go, he's asleep. Let's not wake him."

"Sam," shouted the sheriff, as he moved further into the house. "Let's look back here," he said, as he walked toward the bedroom.

A few seconds later they switched on the light and found Sam lying fully dressed on his bed. He didn't stir as the sheriff said, "Sam! Sam! Are you okay?" At the same time, the doctor took Sam's limp wrist in his hand. There was a faint pulse. He put his hand on Sam's forehead. "He looks flushed," he said softly. "Feels like he has the flu that's all over town. He's burning up with fever."

The sheriff moved closer and said, "I can smell smoke, can't you, Doc?"

"Yeah, it must be on our clothes," replied the doctor.

The sheriff spoke again, "Sam, can you hear me?" There was no response. "Sam, have you been over to the Gentrys'?"

"What are you talking about, Sheriff?" the doctor asked. "This man's one of my patients. He can hardly walk."

The sheriff leaned down so his face was only a foot away from his old friend and asked, "Sam, did you go to the Gentrys'?"

"What's wrong with you, Sheriff? I told you he can't walk much, and he's sick, and besides, when we drove in here I noticed that there wasn't a single track out there in the snow."

An almost indistinguishable smile crossed Sam's face. A smile that only someone like the old sheriff could have seen. Then his head fell to the side. Sam Edwards had died. The doctor placed his fingers around Sam's wrist, and after a few seconds he said: "He's gone. The flu didn't do it on its own. My best guess is his old ticker just plain gave out on him."

"Maybe too much strain?" the sheriff asked.

"No, just too much age," the doctor said.

Near two in the morning, the sheriff had the Gentrys settled in at the local motel. Warren Anderson from the mortuary had come an hour earlier and had taken Sam's body away. Now the sheriff came back to Sam's house. There was something he felt he had to know.

Sheriff Durrant parked his car just in front of the dark and quiet house. In his heart he felt certain that in some miraculous way Sam had gone to the burning house. Soon he would know. Were there tracks out back and across the field? Had Sam saved the boy and brought the greatest joy a family could ever know?

As the old sheriff's boots crunched into the cold snow, he felt for a moment he could hear the angels singing. He paused and looked up at the stars.

He spoke softly as he looked up. "Oh, heck, Sam! You and I both know there ain't no tracks out there. Besides, I need to be home. It's Christmas."

As the sheriff opened his car door, he looked back at Sam's house. He'd miss his old friend. A tear ran down his cheek, and he felt he heard Sam's voice saying, "I finally did it, Sheriff. Merry Christmas."

Already there was a rumor in town that the life of a little child had been saved by a miracle. Sheriff Durrant felt satisfied with that.

The Christmas Marble

By George Durrant

Chapter 1

Most everyone thought Howard Carter was the biggest liar who ever lived in the small town of Rooster Creek. He told stories that were hard to believe, but the way he told them they were hard *not* to believe.

On Halloween Day of 1940, in Miss Dunyon's fifth grade class, he stood up in front of us and said, "See this here marble?" He held it up high between his thumb and first finger. His eyes sparkled with excitement and he smiled a sinister smile as he declared, "This marble is the marble of death. Whoever owns it will die. I got it from Egypt—from King Tut's tomb. It's cursed just like all that other stuff you've heard about that came from that haunted place."

Howard's eyes swept across the room and focused on me, Jake Mobley. I was scared of stuff like that and he seemed to sense my fear. Suddenly he moved his arm forward and faked like he was throwing the marble to me. He shouted, "Catch it, Jake!" I about had a heart attack. It was worse than the day the bully Bobby Jackson wrapped a live water snake around my neck.

Bobby, who was known for speaking up without raising his hand, shouted, "You're a liar, Howard. Nobody believes your dumb stories. You didn't get that from a tomb."

Miss Dunyon, our teacher, stood up like she always did when her feathers had been ruffled and shouted, "Bobby, we don't call each other liars. And if you want to say something, raise your hand."

Bobby laughed. He didn't pay much attention to what she or anybody else said. He couldn't spell, or do long division, or draw, or recite his multiplication tables. But he still thought that he knew everything about everything. He sat in the back. Miss Dunyon had him sit back there because he was so big. Bobby had moved to Rooster Creek three years ago. His parents had joined the Mormon Church in Georgia and had come west to be with the Saints.

Bobby was angry that they had to come to Rooster Creek. He said that he hated living here and wanted to move back to the South where the boys were not a bunch of sissies like they were in Utah.

Howard, who was not fazed by Bobby's outburst, continued, "Just before I was born, my dad said to my mom, 'Look at this headline. It says, *HOWARD CARTER ENTERS KING TUT'S TOMB.*'"

"My dad read the whole article and announced, 'I reckon we are related to Howard Carter since our name is Carter. Besides,' he said, 'Our family came from England, and that is where the explorer came from.'

"The next day, my dad sent Mr. Carter five dollars in the mail and asked him to send him something from King Tut's tomb. The day I was born this marble came in the mail and so my dad named me Howard Carter. Just like the explorer."

Bobby let out a big burst of laughter and Miss Dunyon stood up and glared at him until he was silent.

Howard continued, "My dad loved this marble. He was carrying it in his pocket the day he got killed in a car accident."

Bobby couldn't restrain himself and shouted out, "That marble ain't cursed and didn't have nothin' to do with your dad dying."

Howard smiled, looked straight at him, and replied, "So, you think it ain't true? Then maybe you'd like to take this here marble home with you, Mr. Tough Guy."

"I got enough marbles already," Bobby replied in a more quiet voice.

"Just listen and let Howard tell the story," Alta Hall said as she glared at Bobby.

Bobby glared back but then knew he couldn't win a staring contest with Alta. All of us boys were scared of Bobby but Alta wasn't. He looked away and spoke out real loud. "What you're saying ain't true because they didn't have no marbles in Egypt."

Howard smiled without opening his mouth. He replied, "They sure did. It's right there in the encyclopedia."

Miss Dunyon walked over to the bookshelf. As she bent down to get the encyclopedia from the shelf the sun was coming in the window and lighted the edge of her yellow hair. I thought she was real pretty, but I decided she must not be because she wasn't married. She opened the "M" book, turned to "Marble," and read, "Marbles is a children's game played with little balls of many colors. It is a very old game. Egyptian and Roman children played with marbles before Christ was born."

Bobby slumped down in his seat and murmured, "What do they know?"

Miss Dunyon put her hand on Howard's shoulder and said, "Well, as usual, Howard is right."

A smug smile filled Howard's face. He loved to prove he was smarter than the rest of us. He again held the marble out between his finger and thumb and said, "If you get this marble, give it back to me. Don't throw it away or lose it. Don't give it to somebody else. You have to give it back to me so I can send it to the explorer. Then he can put it back in the tomb. If you get it and don't give it to me, then don't blame me for what happens."

Silence filled the room. Howard stood there as his eyes slowly swept from one of us to the next. Finally he put the marble in his pocket and started back to his seat by putting his right leg out and then dragging the left one up even. This was his way of walking since his left leg had been paralyzed by polio two years before.

As Howard passed by me, he looked down and smiled. His coal black hair that stuck out from his head like porcupine quills, made his face look white as milk. He looked sick. After he sat down right by my side, I could hear him breathing like he'd just run up the Star Flour Mill hill. He was gasping like he might not make it to his next breath. Then he started coughing like he had a kernel of popcorn caught in his throat. No matter how hard he coughed, he couldn't get it out.

I started thinking that the cursed marble had caused all Howard's sickness. I moved to the other side of my seat to get as far away from the marble as I could.

Howard, who missed coming to school a lot because of sickness, didn't ever talk about the marble again. As time passed, my schoolwork and my chores at home kept me so busy that by Thanksgiving I almost forgot all about the dreaded marble.

Chapter 2

December is my favorite month and finally it was here. I liked to spend most of my time sleigh riding, building snow forts, and just thinking about Christmas. I loved Christmas. I always got Tinker Toys, but this year I had my heart set on getting a giant Erector Set. I knew I could build a lot more stuff with it than with Tinker Toys. I'd seen the set I wanted in the toy section of the J.C. Penney store. It was the biggest set they make. I told Mom I hoped I'd get it. She said she'd ask Dad if he thought Santa Claus could get me one. I wondered why she still believed in Santa Claus.

The cold and snowy days of December passed real slow. The Rooster Creek fire department hung about a hundred strands of colored lights across Main Street. Dad and Mom and me rode downtown in the Model A car to have a look. I'd never seen anything so bright and pretty. The week before the big day I went with Dad up the canyon to cut a tree. I did most of the decorating—the icicles and all. Every night as I lay in bed in my back bedroom I'd drift off to sleep dreaming of my Erector Set.

Finally it was the last week of school before the Christmas break. As I walked to school through the newly fallen snow I was wondering who in my class would pick my name in the gift exchange drawing. I hoped Alta Hall would get it. I knew she'd get me something real good. I hoped Bobby Jackson didn't get it because he said whoever's name he got was just going to get a lump of coal.

Bobby was always saying stuff like that and nobody dared talk back to him. His grip was stronger than a vise. He didn't smile much. He had a stare that was real stern. He could make anybody blink in two seconds if they tried to have a staring contest with him. Not even Miss Dunyon would look directly into his eyes. He was the boss of the playground. His hair was cut real short so that he never had to comb it. He didn't have a neck that could be seen, but it must have been there to keep his head on. In the winter he wouldn't wear a coat. In the summer he wouldn't wear a shirt and you could see his muscles.

Miss Dunyon had us all put our names in a small box. Howard was not there and so she put his name in for him. Then we each took turns and pulled one name out and secretly read it. I got the name of Val Storrs. I was glad to get his name because I knew he liked to go deer hunting with his father. So I'd get him a three powered spy glass that I'd seen for fifty cents at Chipman's Merc. He'd be able to see a deer a mile a way with that. I watched real close to see who got my name, but I couldn't tell because everybody was as secret as Dick Tracy, the detective in the comic section of the *Deseret News*. Miss Dunyon told us Howard was getting more sick all the time and that she would take out a name and go visit him and give it to him so him and his mom could send a gift for that person.

The next day we each brought our gifts all wrapped up real fancy and put them under our cardboard Santa Claus. There was a name on the outside of each gift telling who it was for. But there was no way to tell who it was from. It was Friday, the last day of school, and then we'd be out for Christmas that was coming up on Wednesday. We didn't do much schoolwork that day and I was glad because I couldn't think of nothing except the gift that I was about to get. That, plus the Erector Set, was going to make this my best Christmas so far. I could hardly wait for the time when Miss Dunyon would pass out the gifts.

Finally she got started but it seemed like it was taking forever. Almost everybody got theirs before she finally handed me mine. It was in a box that cherry chocolates come in, but by shaking it I could tell it wasn't chocolates. At first I thought it was just a bunch of crunched up newspapers. I quickly pulled them all out and threw them over my shoulder. Then I saw the most beautiful marble I had ever laid eyes on. I loved playing marbles and when I saw that glistening glass marble my heart skipped a beat.

Bobby Jackson shouted to me, "Jake, What did you get?"

"A real good marble," I replied.

Bobby walked up and said, "Let me see it." I could tell that he was wishing he had got it because he was the best marble player in school. He held it like he was going to shoot it. Then he looked at it again and said, "I've never seen a marble like that."

Alta Hall was looking over my shoulder as Bobby handed back my marble. She said softly, "It looks like that marble Howard told us about from King Tut's tomb."

Suddenly everything changed. All the happiness of looking forward to Christmas drained out of me like air out of my bike tire when I ran over a broken Coke bottle. I just sat there staring at the marble.

Just then the bell rang and two seconds later all the kids were out of the room and running toward the fire station to line up for the sack of candy and nuts and the orange that the fireman gave out each year. I just sat there holding the marble. "'What's wrong, Jacob?" Miss Dunyon asked.

"Nothing," I replied softly as I got up and slowly made my way out of the classroom. I had planned to try to be first in line at the fire station and then go on downtown to look at the Erector Set at Penny's. Now candy and nuts and even Erector Sets didn't matter anymore.

I ran all the way home. Without even going in the house, I pulled my bike off the porch and headed for Howard's house as fast as I could pedal. As I was crossing Main Street, I was thinking of the marble so much that I rode right out in front of a car.

It slid to a stop and Mr. Boley shouted out, "Watch out! Do you want to get killed or something?"

I rode away without looking back because I knew the marble was trying to take its toll. When I arrived at Howard's house, I was excited to be standing on his porch. I clutched the marble for what I knew would be the last time. Soon Howard would come to the door, I'd reach out and give the marble to him and that would be that. I'd be safe again.

I rang the doorbell and anxiously waited, but no one answered. I rang it again and no answer. I knocked real loud and no one came. I knocked louder and nothing. Where was he? Where was his mother? I waited on the porch for nearly a half-hour and nobody came. I knew I had to get home to gather the eggs just as I did every night.

After supper, I rode back to Howard's. When I rode through town I didn't even look up at the Christmas lights that hung over Main Street. I usually loved looking at those lights but not tonight. I knew Howard would be home by now. He had to be. I knocked loud enough to be heard all over the house. I waited for some noise inside, but there wasn't any. I frantically pounded on the door like I was TJ Turner, the town cop. Still no one came. On the porch I walked in a small circle for at least ten minutes and then I knocked again. No answer. I could feel the marble bulging in my pocket.

It was starting to snow. I loved snow. But not now. Now I hated it. I hated it almost as much as I hated Howard Carter. Why did he have to give me the marble? I sadly returned home.

My mom and dad went to bed and told me to do the same. I didn't want to go to bed. I just wanted to sit as close as I could to my mother's bedroom door. She finally came out and made me go to bed. I wanted to tell her why I was so scared, but I felt if I did, it might cause the curse to switch to her. I went to my own room and left the light on because I knew that a curse works best in the dark. I lay there on my back looking up at the ceiling. Every sound in the night made me tighten my muscles in fear. I started thinking about my grandfather dying and how when they were carrying him out of our house in a big basket his arm fell over the side and his dead hand dragged across my legs. I remembered that every time I heard that somebody died. I hated people dying. Most of all I would get sick at heart if I ever thought of my mom dying. Somehow I finally fell asleep.

It was now Saturday morning, and I was almost out of my mind with fear.

After breakfast I rode back down to Howard's house. It was hard to ride through the six inches of snow but I didn't think of that. I had to get to Howard's as fast as I could. I knew time was running out.

As I leaned my bike against the pine tree by his house, I saw a sight that I'll never forget in a million years. There, coming around the corner, was the big black funeral car with the undertaker Herman Henderson steering it right toward where I was standing. I ran and jumped on my bike and was out of there in a split second. I knew Herman was coming for me. It took all the courage I had to look back. The big black hearse had stopped. It had stopped right in front of Howard's house. Then it hit me. Howard had died. "Oh no!" I said to myself. "Now there is no way to return the marble. What can I do?"

As I slowly pedaled home I was too sad about myself to even think of Howard Carter dying. That cold December day was the darkest day of my life. Not once that morning or afternoon did I think of the Erector Set. Christmas never once came to my mind. I still had the marble and there was no way to get rid of it. Finally night came.

I laid in bed worrying more than ever before. Then I had the most horrible thought I had ever had, "Maybe the marble would not get me—instead it would get my mother." I put my head under my pillow and began to cry.

Chapter 3

When I woke up it was Sunday morning. I was glad because I knew that curses didn't dare do much work on Sundays.

Brother Schmidt, our Sunday School teacher, asked us why Christmas was such an important day.

Alta replied, "Because that is the day Christ was born." She then started to cry a little bit as she continued, "I don't know if you heard or not, Brother Schmidt, but Howard Carter died." She started to cry even more as she said, "I'm so glad that because of Jesus, Howard will be all right."

Brother Schmidt was silent. He looked at each of us as his eyes glistened with tears. As his eyes met mine, I wanted to tell him that next week he'd be crying about me dying. Or worse still, about my mother dying. But I couldn't say anything.

Then Brother Schmidt opened his scriptures and read, "As in Adam all die, even so in Christ will all be made alive." He then explained that because of what Adam did, all of us would take turns dying. He smiled and added, "The good part is that because of what Christ did, everyone will come back to life." He then read, "Let not your heart be troubled. Neither let it be afraid." Somehow for just a minute I felt peace. But then fear came back as I thought, "They all love Howard, but I hate him. Because of what he did my mother or me is going to die. And Jesus or nobody else can do anything to stop that."

After Sunday School, Bobby, Alta, and me were walking home. Bobby hated it when Alta walked home with us. He'd never let her do it on school days, but on Sunday we all came out the same door of the church. So there wasn't any way to get rid of her. I liked her to walk with us, but I didn't say that to Bobby. That day I didn't say anything to anybody.

Bobby finally asked me, "Why are you acting so quiet?"

I didn't answer.

Alta asked, "Is it because of Howard dying?"

I didn't want to say nothing but all of a sudden I blurted out, "I still got that marble and I know what is coming."

Bobby did the worst thing he could have done—he started to laugh. Then he said, "You worried about that curse stuff? That is all a bunch of bull just like everything Howard said."

Alta interrupted, "Jacob knows Howard made up that story. Don't you, Jacob?" I didn't answer.

To get home we had to pass right in front of the mortuary. Bobby said, "Look, Jake, there is a dead guy in there holding a marble." He laughed because he knew I was scared to look in.

Alta said, "That isn't a dead guy—it's Herman Henderson sitting in his office chair." I still didn't look in because seeing the town undertaker was as bad as seeing a dead guy.

Herman Henderson, the town undertaker, had assisted his father until the elder undertaker died. Since then, Herman had been in charge of the whole business. He was the tallest man in Rooster Creek. He was hunched over because ever since he was a teenager he had tried to appear shorter.

My dad told us at dinner one night, "Herman could have been a good basketball player in his younger days, but he was too clumsy. He is still the clumsiest man in the county. Go to any funeral and you'll see him almost fall in the grave. One of these times he will fall in and they'll bury Herman instead of the dead guy." Then my dad laughed and laughed.

My mom replied, "Don't make fun of him. He is the kindest man in town."

Dad replied, "Huh! If he is so kind why can't he find a wife?"

"Maybe he will someday," Mom said.

"His chances of getting married are about the same as the old maid school teacher Miss Dunyon."

"The school board will fire Miss Dunyon if she gets married," Mom said.

My dad answered, "No one would marry an undertaker with a voice lower than a fog horn."

Mom defended him again. "He talks real low to people who are sad so he can seem as sad as they are."

Dad continued, "The only real talent he has is never smiling."

Mom added, "I saw him smile once. It's just that he knows if he smiles somebody will think that he doesn't care about their sorrow. If that happened they might go over to Pineville to get the undertaker over there to bury their loved one."

As we were nearly past the mortuary, Bobby said, "The undertaker is pointing at you saying, 'I'll be to your home before you can say Afra Cadaver.'"

His words were scaring me, so I shouted, "Shut up!"

"You know that stuff bothers him," Alta added. I was glad that someone else understood how I felt.

When we got to Bobby's house his mother was standing in the doorway. She called out, "Hi Jacob. Was Sunday School good?"

"Yeah," I replied.

Then she said, "Merry Christmas, Jake."

Because of her sickness she looked like she was nothing except skin and bones. When Bobby went up to her, she hugged him. Bobby was a bully at school, but his ma didn't know that. If she had known that it would have broken her heart. She thought he was a real good boy.

After Sunday dinner I felt a little better. I decided to walk down to the old mill lane. I loved that place more than any other place in the world. I loved to look at the trees that grow tall on both sides of the curved dirt road. Snow clung to the limbs and branches and made them look like they had been decorated for Christmas. I liked to hear the little stream as it passed over the rocks. There was a lot of ice here and there, but there were a lot of places where I could still see the dark, sparkling water. I liked to stand on the bridge and look down at where the water came out from under the road. It was dark and deep there and the ice was only over by the edge.

I reached in my pocket and felt the marble. It felt so smooth it was almost slick. I pulled it out and held it in the palm of my hand. As I gazed at it I could see to its very center. I wondered how anything so beautiful could be so bad. I held my hand out over the water. All I would have to do was turn my hand over and the marble would be gone forever. I stood that way for several seconds. I couldn't do it. I remembered what Howard had said. My fingers closed over the marble. I pulled it back, put it in my pocket, and headed for home. In my mind I could hear the words of Brother Schmidt, "Let not your heart be troubled. Neither let it be afraid." I felt better for a minute as I looked up through the snow-covered branches of the trees and could see the pure blue sky. For just a minute I thought about Christmas, but not about the Erector Set.

Chapter 4

Mom took me to Howard's funeral. When we entered the door of the church, my mind wasn't on Howard being dead. It was on his marble. Flowers were everywhere and everybody was dressed in real dark clothes. I felt someone grasp my hand. It was Howard's mom. Her eyes were real red. My mom said to her, "Jacob was in Howard's class."

"Oh, I know Jacob. Howard told me all about how you were so good to him. How you loved to play marbles with him when the other kids wouldn't."

I was scared now more than ever because I knew from what she said that she knew I had the marble, and that I'd be cursed like Howard. I wanted to give her the marble, but she'd already had her share of sadness. I moved forward.

We went into the chapel and waited for the funeral to begin. Miss Dunyon was sitting right next to me. I was glad of that because I liked her. The undertaker wheeled Howard's coffin in from the foyer. It was covered with flowers. I ducked down a little and bowed my head when Herman Henderson was right at my side. He fixed his eyes right in my direction and winked. I looked away real fast toward Miss Dunyon. Her face was red like she was blushing.

The coffin was resting up front and Howard's mom had sat down on the front row. The bishop stood up and told about how much he loved Howard and his mom. Then the school principal, Mr. Larsen, told us that he was named after Abraham Lincoln and that "Abe Lincoln would have liked Howard because Howard never told a lie."

Then Mary Plum, the biggest lady I had ever seen, sang a song about Howard being in the garden alone while the dew was still on the roses. The words she was singing said that Howard was walking and talking with God. I somehow knew that she was right.

When I got home Bobby was standing there. He asked, "How was it?"

"Okay," I answered.

"What did they say?"

"They said Howard was in Heaven walking and talking to God."

"Liars don't go to heaven."

"Maybe he didn't lie. The principal said he didn't lie or do nothing bad."

"That story about the marble was the biggest bunch of bull to ever hit Rooster Creek."

"That wasn't bull."

"It sure was."

"Oh yeah?" Before knowing I was going to, I reached in my pocket and pulled out the marble. Bobby jumped back. His eye was twitching. To make him even more nervous, I held the marble out toward him and said mockingly, "It's yours—take it home."

He backed up even more and said, "I don't need no more marbles. I've got to head for home."

He walked away like he was in a hurry. For just a minute I was glad I had that marble.

That afternoon, Mom asked me to go down to the other end of town and stay at my grandma's so that Aunt Jane could go do her Christmas shopping. I didn't say much to Grandma because the marble made it so all I could think about was when the curse would swing into action. Finally Aunt Jane came back to Grandma's and I headed for home.

As I turned the corner by Lizzie Steggel's house, I shuddered. There, parked two blocks ahead, was the long, black car—the hearse with curtains in the windows. I remembered Bobby's words, "The undertaker is in charge of death in our town." I wished that there was no such person as Herman Henderson in Rooster Creek.

The only car in town big enough to have a dead body in the back was parked smack dab in front of Bobby Jackson's house. Sadly and suddenly I knew that Bobby's mom had died. She was always so nice to me. I felt like crying, but crying was for times when I stubbed a toe or cut a finger. Crying wasn't a big enough thing to do when I knew Bobby's mom had died.

I hoped more than I'd ever hoped anything that Mr. Henderson would never park the hearse in front of my house, but with the marble in my pocket I knew it would park there soon.

My hand grasped the hated marble. I thought of throwing it a mile, but that would only hasten the end. Now I was right beside the long, black hearse. I couldn't look as I remembered seeing the undertaker at Howard's funeral. I was petrified that if I looked toward the house I might see him again. If I saw Bobby's dead mom being carried out in a basket, I'd have been too weak to keep walking.

When I was past Bobby's place I started to run. I had to see my mom.

She was standing over by the stove on the other side of the big kitchen. She turned toward me and I could see an unnatural smile. Her eyes were wet and I knew she knew about Bobby's mom. My mom liked Bobby's mom a lot. They had always walked to church together before the sickness.

She tried to sound cheerful. "Herman Henderson called me and asked if I could help out. I'm making them this chicken noodle soup." When mom said the name "Herman Henderson" my mouth felt dry and stiff inside. She continued, "He said before he took her body to the funeral parlor that he'd come up and take the soup to their house."

"In that car he drives to get dead people?" I asked with pure fear.

"He'll be here any minute."

The inside of my head spun around like a top. I never wanted that thing in front of my house. I hurried out the door and down into the cellar, got the two wire baskets and headed for the chicken coops. Out there I wouldn't see what I never wanted to see.

I slowly gathered the eggs. Before I headed back to the house, I peeked around the corner of the last coop to make sure. I was relieved to see it wasn't there.

As we ate our soup we didn't say anything except, "Pass the salt and pepper," and stuff like that. Finally Mom said to Dad, "When Herman came by he asked me if Bobby could come up here and sleep tonight. Brother Jackson is too broken up to take care of him."

My dad nodded his approval. I wanted to say something against it, but I didn't. It was just that I didn't like Bobby coming up to my house to spread his sorrow all over our place. Besides, with losing his mom and all, he might be on one of his mean streaks.

Bobby's dad knocked. When Mom opened the door, I could see Brother Jackson looking down. I heard him say, "Here he is." Then his dad was gone. There stood Bobby like he was the loneliest kid in the whole world. Mom put her hand on his shoulder and gently invited him to come inside. As he entered she said, "Thanks for coming. I loved your mother, and I love you."

Bobby looked over at where I was sitting listening to the radio. I looked back for a second and then I looked away. I didn't feel like I could stand to look at a boy whose mom had just died. I knew how he felt. Mom took his coat and hung it on the same nail in the hall that mine was hanging on. Then she said, "Bobby, you can listen to *Jack Armstrong* on the radio with Jacob. He listens every night."

"I do, too," Bobby said in a soft voice.

Mom pulled a kitchen chair over close to mine, and Bobby sat down. He didn't say, "Hi" or anything, and I didn't either. Soon we both forgot that the other one was even sitting there because Jack Armstrong and his brother Billy had just been captured by some head-hunting, no-good savages.

This all happened in the deepest part of the African jungle. The program ended just as the natives were about to run a spear into the All-American Boy. I was so scared for Jack and his friends that I forgot all about Bobby's mom dying. Bobby did, too. When the announcer started talking about eating Wheaties, I asked Bobby what he thought would happen to Jack and them next.

He answered, "Them good natives that Jack helped down the river will come and rescue him and his brother."

I liked what he said. "That's just what I was thinking," I replied.

A little while later we were listening to *Hop Harrigan,* the ace airplane pilot. The guy at the control tower said, "Control tower to CX4, all clear." Then both Bobby and me said at the same time, "Okay! This is Hop Harrigan coming in." We both laughed because we said it together like that. I felt good listening to the radio with someone who liked the same radio shows that I did.

My mom asked us if we would like to help her make some popcorn balls. "Yeah," I said, and Bobby got up from his chair to show he liked the idea, too. Mom let us put the sugar and vinegar and water in the pan. I let Bobby put in the red food coloring, even though that was the part I always did.

Bobby knew how to make popcorn balls just right. As he was patting one together like a snowball, he said, "Ma and I make these a lot."

After he said that, I looked at him and he looked at me. Then he looked down at the table, and so did I. After we each had gobbled up about three and a half popcorn balls, my mom told us we'd have to go to bed.

She told Bobby he could sleep with me in my bed. I wished she hadn't said that. I hoped Bobby would sleep on the floor in the parlor. It was all right to be with him when my mom was there, but I didn't want to be alone with him.

When we were in bed, Mom turned out the light. We just laid there not saying anything to each other. I was thinking about how Bobby was feeling. I knew he must be thinking about his mom being gone. Everything seemed sadder because it was dark. I wanted to go to sleep so I wouldn't have to think about anything, but I couldn't. Then through the darkness I could hear Bobby crying, really soft like. Hearing him doing that made me sadder than I'd ever been before.

I wasn't thinking about my feelings; I was thinking about his. I wanted to say something, but I didn't know what to say. I hoped Bobby would start sleeping so he'd stop crying. It seemed like an hour went by and he just laid there crying.

Then, without thinking, I said, "I'm sorry your mom died."

"Me too," he answered.

Seemed like right after that, I could tell that Bobby was asleep.

Chapter 5

The next morning Mom made hot cakes and both me and Bobby covered them over with a whole lot of strawberry jam. Mom usually told me not to put that much on, but she didn't say anything that morning.

I looked over at Bobby who had a look of hope in his eyes. He seemed smaller as he sat at the breakfast table. His face didn't look stern like it did on the school playground and he didn't look like a bully. It seemed as though death was the bully and Bobby was trying to not let it hurt him. I could tell that Bobby needed me, so I was glad to stay with him.

After breakfast I said, "Do you want to go out and play in the barn? It's warm in there even in the winter."

"If you want to," Bobby said meekly.

"Let's go." I quickly opened the back door and bounded out of the house. Bobby was right behind me. We slid down the small hill that was just beyond the coal shed.

We ran at top speed past the outdoor toilet. My heart pounded as we came close to the barn. Being in that place was more fun than being at the Poultry Day Carnival. I opened the creaky door of the big weatherworn barn. We both felt the pure joy of entering that magical place. I didn't think about the marble.

I began to scale the steep side of the haystack. Halfway up, I shouted, "Come on, Bobby, let's climb Mount Everest." Just then my foot slipped back and hit him on the head. I expected to be called a twerp, but instead I heard, "That's okay."

I felt Bobby's strong arm grab my foot and push me up. I reached up and was able to pull myself to the top. Bobby bounded up and the two of us sat together.

"You saved my life, Bobby. I could have fallen a thousand feet into the crevasse."

"Yeah!" Bobby said excitedly. He added, "We are the first human beings to ever set foot on the top."

Bobby looked up at the rafters. He stood, reached up, and grabbed one with both hands. He shouted, "I saw this in the circus when I lived in Georgia."

He pulled himself up and did a summersault on the beam and then dropped down and said, "You try it."

"I can't."

"You can. I'll boost you."

"I can't."

"Come on. Reach up."

Bobby held my ankles and lifted. I grabbed the beam and pulled myself up. "Just hold on and do what I did," Bobby said.

I did the same trick and dropped back down. "Way to go!" Bobby said with pride. "If we had a rope, we could tie it on that rafter and swing down like we were Tarzan."

"There's one in the granary," I told Bobby. "I'll get it."

Soon I was back and I handed him the rope, and he crawled out on the rafter and tied it.

"Try it!" I said.

"No, you go first," he replied, handing me the end. I swung down and tried to make the sound that Tarzan makes, "Ahaahaahah!" I threw the rope back, and Bobby came swinging down and landed beside me. It was the most fun I had ever had on a swing.

While we were playing, we each forgot that Bobby's mom had died. I forgot about the marble. We were laughing because we were the happiest kids in the world. Then Bobby sat on a bale of hay and started to cry.

I knew he was thinking about his mom and wishing he could be talking to her again. I started to think about my mom and about the marble. I could imagine how he felt. I didn't know what to do. I thought that maybe I should go in the house and get some popcorn balls to help him feel better.

Instead of doing that I just sat there on a nearby bale of hay and thought how much Bobby must hurt. I knew how I'd feel if my mom was gone and was never coming back. I gripped the marble in my pocket. After a while, Bobby stopped crying.

I softly said, "Should we dig a tunnel in the hay for a gold mine?" He smiled and soon we were taking turns going in and out of our gold mine.

I said, "We need to hide something in there like it's a big piece of gold or something."

"Good idea!" Bobby said as he reached in his pockets for something we could use.

I waited until Bobby said, "I can't find nothin'. Can you?"

I jerked the marble out of my pocket and held it out in the palm of my open hand.

"It's a beauty, ain't it? Too bad it's cursed. You might lose it."

"We won't lose it."

I then hurried into the cave and came out. "Go find it."

In a few seconds Bobby came back. "That darn marble was sure easy to find." He quickly handed it to me and said, "Let's not play that game anymore."

I climbed to the top of the haystack, swung off, and landed right by the barn door. When my feet hit the ground, I looked up and there standing in the barn doorway was a man in a dark suit.

It was Herman Henderson, the undertaker. I was so surprised and scared to see him that I stumbled backwards. I wanted to climb back up the haystack and be as far away from him as I could get, but I couldn't move a muscle. Bobby swung down and we both stood there looking at him as he stared back at us. I didn't know if Bobby was as scared of him as I was.

Herman smiled and said, "Hello, boys. Mind if I come in and have a look?"

I wanted to tell him to get out of there and never come on my property again. He walked right past us into the barn.

While we were all standing there, he looked all around and said, "I like it in here. You boys sure are lucky on a cold day to have a place to play like this." Then, without even asking if he could, he started climbing up the haystack. "Mind if I have a turn?" he said as he took off his black coat and laid it over a bale of hay.

Neither of us said anything because we were wondering what was going on. He grabbed the rope and with a loud, "Ahaahaahah!" he swung down and nearly knocked me over. "Oh, sorry! I kind of lost my balance there."

We still hadn't said anything to him. He looked around again and said, "When I was your age, my dad had a farm, and we had a barn just like this one.

"Could we talk a few minutes?" he asked as he moved a bale of hay a little way away from another one. He said, "Sit down, guys. Don't be nervous. I'm a real friendly guy." We didn't say he could talk to us, but we knew he was going to anyway.

I didn't want to be sitting there face to face with a man who specialized in dead people. Still, he didn't seem like an undertaker sitting there. He seemed like a normal man.

Herman reached in his pocket and pulled out a bag of pink peppermints. I liked them better than I did any other candy. "Take as many as you want."

I only took four and Bobby took a whole handful. I didn't mind that he got more than me because I had a mom and he didn't. As I was sucking on my peppermint, I forgot that the man who gave it to me was an undertaker.

Mr. Henderson then leaned back on his bale of hay and locked his hands around his uplifted knee. He looked at Bobby and said, "I'm sure sorry about your mother. She was a great lady. She was in a lot of pain because of her sickness. Now she's free from all that and she's happy."

The way he said those things made me feel peaceful like I felt for a little while in my Sunday School class and when Mary Plumb sang about Howard in Heaven walking and talking with God. Somehow I knew that what the undertaker was saying wasn't a lie. The barn suddenly seemed like a church.

He then asked us if we had ever known anybody who had died. I softly replied, "Howard Carter."

"Oh, sure. I think I saw you at his funeral sitting next to Miss Dunyon."

Tears filled Herman's eyes as he said, "That was a tough one. So close to Christmas and all. Howard was such a good boy. When I learned he died, I felt so bad I didn't want to go over to his house. I knew his mother would be sadder than anybody I'd ever seen before.

"Of course his father is. When I got there his mother told me that she would miss her son. Then she told me that she knew he was still alive and was living in a better place with his grandpa and grandma. She told me that she had bought an Erector Set to give him on Christmas morning from Santa Claus. She got it out and gave it to me to give to any boy who I thought might want it. I wanted to say, 'I would sure like it,' but I didn't."

He continued, "Later that night, I was in the mortuary alone with Howard. While I was helping him get ready for his funeral, something inside me said that he was happier now than a kid on the last day of school. That made me feel good, and I knew that Howard was happy."

While Mr. Henderson was saying these things, I moved a

little closer to Bobby. I wanted to be as close to him as I could get. I started to feel that there wasn't anything in the world to be scared of. I loved Bobby and everybody else. I even forgot that I had the marble.

The undertaker asked us about school. He told us that when he was our age he was good at math. He said, "I had a hard time spelling. I once spelled cat: k-a-t." He started to laugh and we did too. I told him how much I liked doing art stuff.

He answered, "I wish that I was good at art. I can't draw a straight line." He then asked, "Will you paint me a happy picture to hang in my mortuary?" I didn't answer.

Bobby said, "My favorite thing at school is recess because I like to play marbles and football."

"Me too," Mr. Henderson replied, "I played touch football for the team that was sponsored by my undertaking school. We were not very good, and each team we played buried us. We were almost victorious in one game. Time was running out and we were behind by one point.

We were almost to their goal line. I was quarterback and I threw a pass into the end zone. The other team intercepted the ball and ran all the way for a touchdown. That put the final nail in our coffin."

It was easy to talk to Mr. Henderson because he was real interested in everything we said.

He turned around and said, "I've been looking at that tunnel in the hay. It reminds me of one I made in the hay in my dad's barn. I pretended it was a gold mine."

When he said that I looked at Bobby.

Suddenly the undertaker stood up and pulled off his black shoes and knelt down. Then, really fast, like a scared gopher, he disappeared into the tunnel until only his feet with red stockings were sticking out.

We smiled as we watched. When he crawled out, he shouted,

"Guess what? I found some gold in your mine." He handed each of us a nickel. He looked strange because his hair was all messed up and filled with hay leaves.

He pulled a yellow comb out of his back pocket and ran it from the front to the back of his hair. Then he brushed off his shirt and pants and sat down on the bale of hay and put on his shoes.

When he put his coat back on it made him look like the undertaker again, but he didn't seem like the undertaker.

I had the feeling that he took more of a liking to Bobby than he did to me. He put his hand on Bobby's shoulder and looked really serious at him saying, "Bobby, your mother was a wonderful lady and she'll always watch over you. Someday you will be with her again. Jesus will see to that. Soon your sorrow won't hurt so much, and you'll be happy again." I wished I could say things like that to Bobby.

The undertaker looked at his watch and said, "I've got to get going. My luncheon at the Optimist Club starts in ten minutes. Oh! By the way, did either one of you want that Erector Set? Or should I give it to another kid?"

I wanted to say I'd like it, but I didn't say anything. Bobby spoke right up, "I'd sure like it."

"Okay, I'll bring it by." I wished I had said I wanted it but I was glad for Bobby. As he went out the barn door the undertaker looked back and smiled and said, "I know it is a sad time but I still hope that you two have a merry Christmas. So long, my friends."

We watched as he climbed across the big gate and ran toward a red car with white tires. There was a woman sitting real low in the car, like she didn't want to be seen. It looked a little like Miss Dunyon, but I wasn't sure. The undertaker jumped in and drove off really fast. I knew he must be rich because he had two cars and nobody else in Rooster Creek did.

I felt in my pocket to make sure I hadn't lost the marble. It was there. I felt sad and glad all at the same time.

Chapter 6

That afternoon, Mom and I arrived at the funeral for Mrs. Jackson real early—Mom liked to do that. After waiting awhile I heard the back door to the chapel open. The bishop stood up at the pulpit and said, "Everyone please stand."

I looked back and saw Herman Henderson come wheeling the casket down the aisle of the church. I didn't dread looking at him now. As he passed by he looked at me. I figured that he wanted to smile, but he knew a funeral wasn't the right place to smile.

Following along behind the casket was Bobby's dad. He was walking real slow and was staring straight ahead. Bobby was holding his dad's hand, and he was crying a little bit. I knew why. I reached out and put my hand into Mom's hand and moved over as close to her as I could.

Alta Hall was on the row in front of me sitting between her dad and mom. I think it was the first time her mom had ever come to the church. Alta was crying and seeing that made me feel like crying. Feeling the marble in my pocket, I sensed that the next funeral would be the saddest of all.

That night Aunt Jane had to go to Salt Lake City to see her daughter and so Mom asked me to go sleep at Grandma's. Us grandkids took turns doing that. I stayed there to help her do some morning chores and I helped her decorate her little Christmas tree. She gave me a dollar bill and told me to have a Merry Christmas as I went out the door to head for home.

As I entered the south end of the old Mill Lane, I could hear the clapping of loud footsteps up around the bend.

I couldn't see up there but I could tell that someone was running at top speed. When he came into sight I could see that it was Bobby. He was shouting, "Jake! Jake! Come on! Come on! Something's wrong at your house. Herman Henderson's big black hearse is parked smack dab in front of your place. This time it's your mom."

I stopped in my tracks, took a deep breath, and held it for a long time. I lowered my head and moved it from side to side. I had known this time would come, and I didn't cry. I closed my eyes to try to shut out my life. Bobby reached out and took my hand and pulled me forward, "Come on! You've got to get home."

It was a warmer day than we had been having and the snow was falling from the tree limbs and trying to finding its final resting place on the ground. All the dread I'd had about death filled my mind with darkness.

Then, without knowing why, I started to run so fast that Bobby couldn't keep up with me. I hoped, "Maybe Bobby is making this up." I passed the Parduhns' house and turned the corner.

I looked up the Alpine Road, and I could see my house. I felt that the hearse couldn't be there. It couldn't be there. As I stared ahead, tears filled my eyes so I could hardly see. My heart sank. It was there. I turned and began to run in the other direction.

Bobby shouted, "Stop! You've got to go home." I ran all the faster. The next thing I knew, his strong arms were around me. "Come on! You've got to go home." I could see tears in Bobby's eyes. Seeing that gave me the courage to turn and slowly head toward home.

I rushed past the hearse without looking at it. Bobby stood at the front gate, and I walked alone up the sidewalk. I climbed the three steps and stood on the cement porch, opened the front door, and entered.

Dad was sitting in the wooden rocking chair that he always

sat in and next to him sat old Doctor Richards. On the other side was Herman Henderson. Dad quickly stood up and came over to me. Tears filled his eyes as he embraced me and held me close.

I began sobbing and Dad pulled back. With his hands on my shoulders he softly said, "Your mom got real sick this morning. She had a terrible pain in her stomach and she just kept getting worse and couldn't breathe. I called Doc Richards, and he said that he would come right up."

By now the doctor and the undertaker were standing on each side of me. Dr. Richards said, "I came up as quick as I could. When I got here I knew your mother was in real trouble. Her throat was so swollen. She was choking to death."

I wasn't listening. I didn't want to hear anymore. I didn't want to live any more. If the marble had to take her I wanted it to take me too.

The undertaker got down on one knee, looked into my eyes, put his hands on my shoulders and said, "Doc Richards came running into my mortuary shouting, 'Herman, I've got to hurry up to Mobleys'. She is real sick.'"

Then Doc broke in and said, "I told Herman that I had tried to start my car and the battery was dead. I asked him to give me a lift up here."

Herman spoke again, "My regular car was in Dave Greenwood's getting fixed and the only car I had was the hearse. We came up the old Alpine Road faster than . . . I mean real fast."

Dr. Richards almost shouted, "I got here just in time. I put a tube in your ma's throat and she started to breathing."

Then Herman slapped his forehead with his open hand and said. "Oh no! I hope you didn't think that your mom had... She's okay now."

Bobby, who had been standing outside, knocked. I opened the door and he asked fearfully, "Is your ma dead or what?"

I joyfully replied, "She's okay." He let out a yell that must have gone clear downtown. He jumped off the porch and ran back down the sidewalk and out the gate as he shouted over his shoulder, "I'll go tell Alta. She loves your ma like I do. She'll be as happy as I am."

I shouted as loud as I could, "Merry Christmas, Bobby. Tell Alta the same."

I hurried to Mom's bedroom door and looked at her laying there. She smiled a big smile. I thought it was like the morning of the first resurrection. I went over and laid down right beside her and she pulled me close to her. I've been happy a lot of times. But I had never been this happy.

Dad came to the door and said, "How you doing now, Marinda?"

She nodded that she was doing fine.

"Doc wants to send up some medicine. Jacob can go back with them and walk home with it."

I was so happy, I would have walked to Salt Lake City and back. As we approached the hearse, Herman said, "I've got a big package on the front seat, so with Doc on one side and me on the other, would you mind riding in the back?"

"It's okay," I said with no fear. I felt like I had just been invited to take a seat on the Ferris Wheel at the carnival.

Herman opened the back door of the hearse and said, "Lay down if you want." The doctor let out a really loud laugh. Alta and Bobby saw me getting in, and they weren't laughing. I waved to them as we drove away. Their eyes were as wide open as silver dollars. I couldn't see good because of the drapes covering the windows, but it looked like they were holding hands. I was sure that they weren't.

I wanted to lay down but I was afraid the curse might think I was mocking it and fly into action. So I sat up as straight as I could.

At the doctor's office, he wrote something on a paper. Herman and I drove to Thornton's Drug and got the medicine.

I turned to begin to walk home when Herman said, "I'll take you."

This time I got to ride up front. I'd never seen the Christmas lights look so bright. I saw some high school kids standing in a group. I rolled down the window and could hear them singing, "Silent Night." It sounded liked angels. I hoped some of the kids along the road would see me so I could wave at them. I saw Myron Briggs and Clifford Laycock walking along by the church. They were looking the other way until Herman honked. They saw me and I waved. They just stood there gawking.

As we rode along, I asked, "Mr. Henderson, what about curses?"

"What about them?"

"Do you believe in them?"

"Yeah, I believe in them. Me being so tall and having size fourteen feet is a curse. I can't find shoes that fit, and my pants are always too short. That's a curse."

"Not that kind. I mean the kind that can cause sad things."

"The greatest curse I know is that Miss Dunyon and I . . . Well, the school board of this darn town won't let her get married, or they'll fire her. Loving a woman and not being able to marry her is the worst curse of all."

"Somebody dying is the worst," I said.

"I used to think that, but I don't anymore. It's sad for the ones left behind, but it teaches us how precious life is and how we ought to love and care. Death is a lot of things but it is not a curse."

Finally he finished, and I spoke, "I mean, do you believe in curses like in the tombs of Egypt and all that?"

Herman then nodded and said, "Oh yeah. Now I see what you mean."

"Do you believe in that stuff?" I asked.

"Movie makers make that up to scare folks. There's nothing to that."

"Do you want to see something?"

"What?" he asked.

I pulled the marble out of my pocket and held it between my finger and thumb. "Wow!" he said. "Where did you get that beauty?" He about drove off the side of the road because he kept staring at it.

I told him that Howard Carter had given it to me for a Christmas present. "Some present!" I said. I then added, "He knew it would get me or my mom."

By now we were pulling up in front of my house. Herman reached out, took the marble and said, "Let me hold that. Wow! Look at that!"

He turned it over and over again in his fingers and asked, "How come this thing is so beautiful?"

"Because it's cursed. Whoever has it will die or someone they love will die."

"Come on, Jacob. You don't believe that."

"It's true. Howard told our class this marble once belonged to King Tut. Howard Carter, the explorer, broke into that tomb. He found this marble. King Tut's spirit was lurking in the tomb and put a curse of death on anyone who took his stuff. Especially this marble that he played with."

"You're kidding."

"It's the gospel truth. Howard's dad got it from the explorer and gave it to Howard. He told our class that if we ever got it to give it back to him or die. I could never give it back because Howard died. The curse got him just like it tried to get my mom."

"Jacob, it wasn't a curse that got Howard. It was polio that ruined his lungs and finally took his life."

I added, "The curse probably got Bobby Jackson's mom by mistake thinking she was my mom. We live in the same neighborhood and the curse might have got the wrong address."

The undertaker started to laugh. He told me to calm down. Then he said, "Bobby's mom has been sick a long time. It wasn't a magical curse that took her. It was the curse of cancer."

"You can say what you want. It's the curse. That's why I got to get it back to Howard. My mom made it this time, but . . ." I then said, "You know about dead people. You got to help me get this back to Howard."

He then held the marble up toward the afternoon sun and said, "I'll do something better than that."

"What?"

"I collect marbles and this is a rare one. Collectors love this kind. I'll give you twenty dollars for it."

"What about the curse?"

"This marble isn't from King Tut's tomb. It was made in a marble factory in North Carolina. I know about marbles. There were only 200 marbles made like this one."

"What about the explorer, and Howard's dad?"

"I wouldn't put much stock in what Howard's dad said. I think Howard told that story about the curse to scare you guys so that none of you would ever take his prized marble. Then when he knew he was going to die he wanted you to have it because you were his best friend. It is the best gift one kid ever gave another. Has anything bad happened to you since you have owned it? Think it over, and if you want to sell it, I'll buy it."

I sat there in silence. Could he be right? He then spoke, "You have to understand, Jake. Death is not a curse. It is a good thing. Oh, sure it is sad.

"But when you know about Jesus Christ and His coming back to life, you know that death isn't the end of those we love. We will see them again. So from now on, Jake, don't let your heart be troubled about death."

I looked over at him and I could feel a peaceful feeling in my heart. Only this time it was lasting longer than it did in Sunday School.

As I got out of the hearse the undertaker said, "Hey! I forgot. Was it you or Bobby who wanted the Erector Set? I can't remember. It's right there in the back, if you want it take it."

I thought for a minute. It was getting dark and a gentle snow was falling. I could see our Christmas tree in the window. I said softly, "It was Bobby who wanted it."

"That's right, I remember now. I'll drop it off to him."

I took a few steps toward the house and then looked back and said, "Merry Christmas, Mr. Henderson."

The undertaker smiled bigger than any Rooster Creeker had ever seen him smile and said, "Merry Christmas to you, Jake."

I smiled and threw the marble up in the air. I looked at it and it fell gently back into my hand. I decided I could glue a string to it and hang it on our tree. I put it in my pocket, ran into the house and called out, "Mom?"

Mom called out to me from her bedroom. I went in and laid by her side. It was the night before Christmas and I was happier than I had ever been. Soon I fell into a peaceful sleep.

Fifty Years Later

Mom died ten years ago, and I, a fifty-nine-year-old man, cried the most part of a whole day. No boy ever had a better mother; and I still miss her. It was an honor for me to prepare her body for burial.

You see, I'm now the undertaker in Rooster Creek. Herman Henderson and I became real good friends. The school board finally changed its policy, and he and Miss Dunyon were able to get married. They named their first little boy Howard Jacob Henderson.

Herman paid my way to the same undertaker school that he attended, and he and I became partners in his funeral home. Herman died about three years ago, and I miss him more than I can say. My dream is to be as good at being the undertaker as he was.

Today, the day before Christmas in Rooster Creek, a young boy died. He was the grandson of Alta and Bobby. Oh yeah, I should tell you that Bobby's dad wanted to move back to Georgia, but Bobby wouldn't go. He became a plumber and eventually became mayor of Rooster Creek. He also served as Bishop. Alta went away to college and became a nurse. They got married right after she graduated.

Tonight the people of the town came to see the seven-year-old for the last time, or I should say, "for a while." Later that night when all the folks had gone home, I went over to his coffin and moved it over closer to the Christmas tree. The little boy's parents had put a small electronic game in his coffin. They got it for him for Christmas. I picked up the Gameboy and turned it on. I opened the boy's small hand and put his finger on the play button. I kissed him on the forehead, told him "Merry Christmas," and closed the lid. I was so grateful for Christmas.

About the Author

George Durrant was born and raised in American Fork, Utah. He has served in many capacities with the LDS Church Educational System. For several years he was the director of Priesthood Genealogy for the Church.

He served for three years as president of the Missionary Training Center in Provo, Utah, and he has taught religion at Brigham Young University.

He is the author of more than a dozen books, including the best-selling *Love at Home—Starring Father* and *Scones for the Heart.* He has also co-authored a book with his son Devin entitled *Raising an All-American.* He is married to the former Marilyn Burnham. They are the parents of eight children.